Slag Ferguson | Book One

Rat Town Blues

A Novel

Brian Kaufman

Black Rose Writing | Texas

This is a work of fiction. Names, characters, businesses, places, events, and incidents are either the products of the author's imagination or used in a fictitious manner. Any resemblance to actual persons, living or dead, or actual events is purely coincidental.

ISBN: 978-1-68513-676-5
LIBRARY OF CONGRESS CONTROL NUMBER: 2025938864
PUBLISHED BY BLACK ROSE WRITING
www.blackrosewriting.com

Printed in the United States of America
Suggested Retail Price (SRP) $19.95

Rat Town Blues is printed in Garamond Premier Pro

*As a planet-friendly publisher, Black Rose Writing does its best to eliminate unnecessary waste to reduce paper usage and energy costs, while never compromising the reading experience. As a result, the final word count vs. page count may not meet common expectations.

Praise for
Rat Town Blues

"Gritty, intense, and immersive; a razor-sharp noir thriller that plunges into the murky depths of corruption and moral ambiguity."
~*The Prairies Book Review*

"Kaufman's descriptive ability is what makes *Rat Town Blues* a standout from the beginning as Ferguson observes his client with the candid drawl of an experienced detective and the colorful metaphors of a poet"
~**Diane Donovan, Senior Reviewer,** *Midwest Book Review*

"Guard your soul and 'buck up' for Kaufman's latest. *Rat Town Blues* reads like Raymond Chandler's *The Big Sleep* meets Don Winslow's *City on Fire*!"
~**Cam Torrens, award-winning author of the** *Tyler Zahn* **suspense series**

"*Rat Town Blues* combines pitch-perfect noir sensibilities with a complex, affecting, and thoroughly modern setting."
~*IndieReader Reviews*

"Neo-noir masterpiece resets the genre with the type of bold creativity that sparks off the pages like muzzle flashes. If the best anti-heroes are like ticking time bombs, then Slag has nuke codes scribbled on the back of his hand."
~**David Buzan, author of** *In the Lair of Legends*

To Caitlin (our True Crime Fan):
Forever Family

Rat Town Blues

Chapter One
Security for Hire

"It is a tremendous act of violence to begin anything. I am not able to begin. I simply skip what should be the beginning."
~Rainer Maria Rilke

The story starts with a beautiful woman walking into a low-rent office. Some schmuck sits behind the desk wearing yesterday's suit, shirt open at the collar, tie pulled aside. The desk is empty except for the phone. There's a clock on the wall, and the only sound the schmuck can hear is ticking—not even his breath, because he's not breathing. He's staring.

I'm the schmuck.

The phone is a cell with a cracked face, hooked to a charger. The clock is a hand-painted souvenir from the Cave of the Winds, a third-tier tourist spot a hundred miles south of here. My suit has a pasta stain on the front. None of these things bothered me five seconds ago. Now, they feel like a rap sheet.

The woman is blonde, of course. She has the long, slender frame of a foxglove flower, complete with bell-shaped earrings. I'd bet the purse she carries costs more than my office furniture. Her hair is pinned against the back of her head, accented by two hair sticks. Not one strand out of place. Makes you want to shake that hair loose and give it a yank.

The lines around the corners of her eyes and mouth say she's in her thirties. But she acts younger. More innocent. It's a convincing act.

"Mr. Ferguson?" she asks. Her voice sings like wind chimes. My eyes find the tiny gap between her front teeth. Nothing obvious—kind of sexy—but enough of a flaw to remind myself she's flesh and blood.

She looks around the room and frowns. The blinds throw shadows across her face.

"Have a seat," I say. This leaves her a choice, since there are two plastic chairs sitting in front of the desk. She takes the one on the right.

"You were recommended to me by Robert Billotte."

When Bobby Billotte touches something, it's usually with his fists. I know because he's a friend. "Robert Billotte. Well, then. Well recommended. What can I do for you?"

She inhales, as if she's about to launch into something she's rehearsed, which she probably has. Hiring someone like me makes people nervous, like going to a therapist, only grimier. This blue-chip blonde is uncomfortable as hell, sliding around on my deluxe office chair like a fried egg in a saucepan. Nothing will make her feel at ease, except maybe me keeping my mouth shut and my ears open.

So, I do.

"I believe my husband is being threatened," she says. "Someone is calling us. At night. Walter leaves the room to talk, and his voice sounds strange. He's concerned. I can tell." Her hands flutter as she speaks, but I catch sight of the rock on her ring finger anyway. She watches me, then folds her hands into her lap. "He's been very tight-lipped. I think he doesn't want to worry me."

I nod at the empty chair. "I notice your husband isn't here."

"He doesn't know I'm talking to you. He wouldn't approve."

He's cheating on her.

"Where are your credentials?" She glances around the room. "Your walls are bare."

I sigh. "I'm not certified. To be a private investigator in Colorado, you have to attend a bunch of classes, most of which don't have anything to do with investigation. Then, you have to pass the Jurisprudence Exam and apply for a license. That's too many hoops for this poodle to jump through."

"You work illegally?"

"Officially, I'm security-for-hire. I'm a Colorado citizen. I have a driver's license and a social security card. That's all you need for security work."

She bites her pink lower lip. "I may need a real private investigator. I need someone who can find out who is threatening my husband. You need a license for that, don't you?"

"Mostly, you need a car. And a computer."

"You don't appear to have a computer."

I tap my cellphone. She still seems skeptical, so I continue. "Tell me how you ended up coming to me. How do you know Mr. Billotte?"

She hesitates before answering. "I needed advice from someone I trust, so I spoke to the parish priest. He's known me since I was a baby. He baptized me. He's also very wise. After I told him my problem, he introduced me to Mr. Billotte, who said you were the right person for the job. He said my problem was the sort of thing you excel at."

Church? That made sense. Bobby was religious about going to church. "Well, why don't we start at the beginning?"

She blushes. "How much do you charge?"

Not the beginning I had in mind, but that's okay. Saves me from bringing up the subject of fees. My hand wants to move, so I let it reposition the cellphone, flush against the edge of the desk. Then, I quote my hourly rate. "I charge for time on the road, mileage, and any expenses. There's a retainer fee, but I won't know the amount until I know more about your case."

She frowns again. I'm beginning to wonder what her smile looks like.

"My rates are damned reasonable, though you might not know that. Like going to an auto mechanic, right? Some men think they can hike the charge on a woman. Not me."

Her gaze darts to the side. "Your rates are comparatively low."

She's been shopping, and I'm not her first choice.

Still looking away, she says, "My husband is an important man. He works for the government, and his decisions affect a lot of people. That means he has enemies. I do not want to give them ammunition by hiring someone who isn't discreet." She tugs at one of her earrings, and I half-expect the little bell to ring.

"Understood." I wish again that I'd worn my other dress shirt, or a polo. Something clean. "Let's get some preliminary information down so I know where to start."

She opens the little purse in her lap and pulls out a piece of paper. She unfolds the typed page and places it in my hands. Names. Addresses. Contact info.

"You came prepared."

The creases at the corners of her eyes beg a question.

"What?" I ask.

She clears her throat. "For someone in the security field, you're not very, um, large." She blushes, which takes the sting out of her words. "I mean, football player sized, you know?"

I smile. "You don't want some guy with gym muscle nosing around your husband, do you? Drawing attention? I'm nondescript."

She smiles. Finally. "Yes, you are."

Now, *I'm* frowning. I glance down at her information and begin to read aloud. "Your name is Kelly Mason. Your husband is Walter Mason, head of Larimer County Health and Environment—"

"I was wrong. You're quite the detective."

Her face returns to a focused expression, but there's a hint of amusement in her eyes. This one is smart. Which means she probably suspects what I'm going to find. "Tell me who might have a grudge against your husband. And who are the other people on your list?"

"Those are his associates. Some in business, some in government." She pauses, leaning forward while lowering her voice. "And they are *all* enemies."

* * * * *

My office is a second story room-and-a-half in a in one of the oldest buildings in Westbrook. There's a shared bathroom at the end of the hall. The alcove that passes for my second room has enough space for a day bed and two bookshelves, so who needs a real apartment, right? Besides, it's trendy to have an office in Old Town. And I'm a trendy guy.

Before leaving to put Kelly Mason's check in the ATM, I poke my head in to check on Sasha. She's fast asleep, so I ease the door closed and head down the stairs.

The front door of the building empties me directly into Old Town Square, a common area, ringed with tiny shops, pavement cafes and flower beds. Purple, red, and blue perennials, bright awnings and table umbrellas paint my way to the bank.

I always notice the flowers. My ex-wife was a florist.

Today, the plaza looks like a carnival. People eating ice cream and carrying balloons. The giant rock fountain near the center of the plaza spills water while a busker with a sax butchers Coltrane. A breath of wind slips past, tasting of baked goods and smoked meat. At the edge of the flower beds, a young kid bangs away on the yellow and blue piano the city put there. He's oblivious to the sax. That's okay—everybody moves to their own music. I stop to enjoy the moment the way you do when the world gives you a Rockwell painting instead of a slap. Then I move on.

By day, Westbrook is a nice town. It used to have a different name. City officials changed the label when they realized that the army officer they'd named their town after killed Native Americans at the Battle of Mud Creek. Now, it's named after Dr. Joseph Henry Peter Westbrook, an early civil rights activist with more than his fair share of first names.

Might have been nice to have a selection of names to choose from. I don't like mine—Mark. A mark is somebody who gets taken in a fixed game. I prefer what my friends call me—Slag. Slag is the waste matter coming from smelting metal. It's white hot, then it's cold and stony. If you step on it, you'll get cut. I got my nickname back in Cleveland (still named Cleveland).

The bank is a few blocks away. There's no hurry—I'm not trying to cover rent or anything. The truth is, I don't spend much, and my weekend gig tending bar would pay all my bills if I'd cut back on beer and books. There's a small nest egg at the bank and a slightly larger one hidden in the office. But once the check is in the bank, the job will be real.

At the ATM, I withdraw a couple of Tubmans and head for the store to buy something for Sasha. That doesn't take long—I buy the same thing every time.

Back at the office, I can tell she's awake. I hear her short, breathy exhalations, like somebody trying to shout through a ventilator. I ease open the door in case she's standing right behind it. "I'm home."

She's pissed. Nobody likes waking up alone. Sasha carries a lot of baggage. I'm patient, used to the idea that she's never going to get over the past. Abuse is ugly.

So are thoughts of revenge. If I had a way to settle with the guy who hurt her, I'd paint my soul black with his blood. But for now, my job is calming her down. Sometimes all it takes is a touch to her cheek, but today, she's not having it.

I produce the bag. She stops still, her eyes questioning.

"That's right, baby," I say. "I was out because I was buying you this." I open the bag and dump the squeak toy onto the bed.

Sasha pounces, snatching the Lamb Chop and attacking the squeaker, making it scream. Then, she pins the toy with her paws and nips at the fur. She's a big girl, and after an hour or two, she's going to gut the thing, pull out the squeaker, and strip the fur down to the mat.

And I'll buy her another.

Sasha is a rescue dog. I found her wandering the alleys behind the bars near the plaza. It was past midnight and I'd been drinking. The alleys gave me a quick angle home, otherwise, I'd never have seen her. She was staggering, blood dripping from an ear that wasn't there. With just a few floodlights to light the alleyway, the blood on her chest wasn't visible yet. But the torn ear was bad enough.

She saw me and huffed. Gave me pause because mean dogs scare me. But Sasha just stared then crumpled to the asphalt. She tried to hold up her head but folded again. I looked around, wondering if she belonged to anybody nearby, but we were alone. A floodlight at the corner of one building gave me a better look at the blood. She was a mess. No dog tags, just wounds.

I crept a little closer to see if she'd tolerate me. She licked my hand.

And that was that.

We visited an all-night vet up at the college, suffered the pompous son of a bitch in a goatee who wanted three years of financials to treat my dog (by then, she was *my* dog), and by four in the morning, I was home with a patched-up pup and what amounted to a second and third rent bill for the month.

The mess on her chest came from a cut near her throat. Someone had performed a sloppy debarking, maybe with scissors or a kitchen knife.

Having already begun the toy's tragic end, Sasha jumps up to lick my face. She's big and clumsy, colored like old custard, and her tongue is the size of a ribeye steak. She coats my face in dog spit. She likes the toy and wants to thank me. She tries to bark—she will always try to bark—but it comes out as a squeak. We hug like two boxers in a clinch, and she spins away, jumping up on the bed.

She's not pretty. But she's beautiful.

On the one and only occasion Bobby Billotte came to my office, Sasha seemed to like him. I've always thought dogs dislike certain people for good reason. Seeing her lick Bobby's hands validated my suspicion that beneath layers of son-of-a-bitch, Billotte had a nugget of goodness in him. "Why'd you name her Sasha?" he asked, rubbing her neck.

I shrugged. "I wanted her to have a stripper's name."

Chapter Two
Two Slags and The Short Goodbye

"Ah, women. They make the highs and the lows more frequent."
~Friedrich Nietzsche

Pardon a brief aside. I'm sitting in a coffee shop—one of the last—typing this on my laptop computer.

Yeah, yeah. I said I didn't have a computer.

And I didn't. But I do now. And that's something you need to understand. There are two of me in this story—the man who was hired by Kelly Mason to find out who was threatening her husband, and the one who is telling you the story now. One is a man sleepwalking after an ugly divorce, and the other is a guy nibbling banana bread in a coffee shop, trying to make sense of the world. Both men are me, but we are not the same.

You might be asking yourself, what does Narrator Slag know that Slag the character doesn't? That would be smart of you.

I'm cursed with a good memory. My thoughts and actions are chiseled in stone. I write for you as if the past were unfolding in front of me. I'm sitting at my keyboard now, but I'm also at the municipal building where Walter Mason works, unaware that I'll be the protagonist in a story a year down the road. I've come to get a closeup look at his face. How does he carry himself? How does he treat the people he works with? Some of that is professional curiosity, but most of the urge is personal.

I want to see the man Kelly Mason married.

His office is on the second floor of the building, close to Old Town, so I plan to stop by with a stupid question. People ask government people stupid questions all the time, so I'll blend in.

At the entrance to the building, the security team places my wallet, keys and phone in a little plastic basket. I set off the metal arch—maybe my belt?—so they pat me down and wave the wand past my crotch. Without a word, they motion me past, placing my basket of goods on the counter. Their silence bothers me, though saying, "Step through, please," and "You can go now" a thousand times a day would make me want to pull out a Glock and shoot myself. They stand, motionless, focusing on points six inches in front of their faces. It's a common expression these days.

Mason's office is easy enough to find. Reception is absent, so I stand in the office entryway, looking impatient and sighing loudly, which is a great way to be ignored. This buys me time to look around. The cramped waiting area has four chairs and an end table with a few women's magazines, a copy of *Sports Illustrated,* and various fliers about public health. A framed sign behind the reception desk reads, "You are important to us. Please take a number."

I wonder why anyone needs a number in an office with four chairs. Apparently, I don't. There's no ticket dispenser.

From the hallway behind the desk comes the voice of authority—a full-throated tone demanding attention—and a moment later, Walter Mason steps into the open.

He's just a shade shorter than me—maybe five-ten. In his forties, judging by his salt-and-pepper hair, combed straight back. He wears a dark suit, silk tie, and a pair of brown Tom Fords. Thick in the middle, but it's the thick that comes with age, not eating. He sees me, glances around, and upon realizing he's without the buffer of a receptionist, he steps back into the hall, calling for someone named Simone.

Simone, a thin, mousy woman with straight brown hair, comes rushing in. She whispers, "I was in the bathroom," which seems to confuse Walter. Perhaps good employees hold their bladders until after the shift is over. He points in my direction, and she nods, smoothing the wrinkles from her blouse as she heads my way. "May I help you?" she asks.

"I need to speak to Mr. Mason."

"Do you have an appointment?"

"No, but I'm right here, and he's right there." I point. "So, let's do this."

Her face pinches shut. "I'm sorry. Mr. Mason only meets by appointment. What is this regarding?"

Walter Mason watches for a moment from the hallway, then sniffs the air and turns back to his office.

In the end, my plans fail. Even my carefully crafted stupid question goes unused. I leave in a huff, which is how frustrated people react to the rock wall of bureaucracy. Five minutes from now, my face will be a shadowed memory, replaced by the next angry citizen.

In the meantime, I've fixed Walter in my mind. I know his gait—an odd, mincing step that could mean his Tom Fords are too tight. I know his puffy, clean-shaven face. If I hear it again, I'll recognize that haughty, born-to-rule voice.

Mission accomplished, with a bonus. Always meeting by appointment means there's an appointment book. And if good old Walter is cheating, he'll have a phony appointment listed to cover any rendezvous.

I hope Simone and I can be friends.

* * * * *

Back at the office, I plug my cellphone in to charge and click Walter Mason's various social media pages. People share an astonishing amount of data about themselves. At a very minimum, they reveal how they wish to be regarded. They list their friends. They may list their interests. Their causes. And some people spill their darkest secrets, trading candor for "likes."

I write my case notes on spiral notebooks, purchased in bulk from the office supply store at the other end of town. Old notebooks are stored in a plastic tub under my bed. My filing system is the envy of investigators everywhere.

Points of interest—Walter Mason is proud of his record protecting the public. His public safety triumphs are listed. Every few posts, someone (either Walter or an assistant), slips in a family picture to remind everyone that Walter is a human being, not a bot. A few of the pictures show his wife, Kelly. I right click them and save them in a file.

I scour all of Walter's posts, looking for comments, searching for trolls who might be enemies. Names go in my notebook.

I check my phone apps, including my public records app. Folks in the industry use a variety of computer programs, but I stick to phone apps because they're fast.

Besides, I don't have a home computer. Yet. With iPhone version 205, or whatever number they're up to, why spend twice the money?

I start the long process of researching every female friend on Mason's social media. If he's cheating on his beautiful wife, the chances are, the other woman is a media "friend." Since he's a cheat, the other woman will want to keep tabs on him via the Internet.

What kind of woman would Walter Mason chase? His wife is a blonde. Classy and reserved. Smart. Would he look for someone completely different? A wild brunette? Redhead with tats?

I study every female contact on the list. Plain, political, or passionate. Check them all.

I note the time on my Cave of the Winds clock. After six. I've been crouched over the tiny screen for too long. My back feels like four hours of gardening. I log the time in my notebook and sit back.

It's Friday.

I am a creature of habit, diligently working the weekdays as if security was a real job, not a hobby. If I don't, the days will slip away. And, I tend bar every Saturday, which makes Friday my one night out.

I'm in my mid-thirties, but I'm in good shape. I don't eat all that much. I can cook, of course. Tried-and-true recipes like Ramen with a chicken leg, and skillet pasta with ground meat and cheese, but these things take too much time. So, meals get skipped. On Friday, I dine out. I drink and spend time with Bobby Billotte.

It's still hot outside, but a breeze runs along Main Street. The 20-minute walk to the Tap-and-Wing is a pleasant end to my workday. I pass people with their dogs, smiling and carrying poop bags. Kids on skateboards skim the space between me and serious injury with unconscious expertise. But the trip isn't quite the painting Old Town Square presents. Every other shop along the way is empty, which is sad. I remember when Old Town thrived, but the world is winding down now.

The Tap-and-Wing is a small pub on Main Street, with a huge patio, which explains why they're still in business. Bars and restaurants without space can't operate. The Tap has thirty different beers and ten different types of wings, including turkey wings and the legendary Habanero Suicide, which is what I order every single Friday. No way anyone could finish a basket. Good for my mouth and good for my waist.

It's early, so there should be seating left inside. Sure enough, Bobby Billotte sits at a high-top table with a strawberry blonde. Neither one of them is smiling. Bobby is staring at the tabletop with a sullen look nailed to his face.

I've known Bobby for a decade, and in that time, he's had at least twenty girlfriends. Some are young and innocent. Pretty little things with good hearts who end up horrified by him. Some are smart, and they realize his limitations and move on. Some are older—like the gal he's with now—often divorced, with baggage of their own. Bobby's sardonic side appeals to them, and they last longer. One even lasted a year. When she pushed for a more permanent relationship, he dropped her like Clay dropped Liston in Lewiston—which is to say, he never hit her, but she went down just the same.

Yes, that was a boxing reference. I'll do that on occasion. I was a boxer once. If you don't get the joke, don't worry. Just assume it was clever and move on.

The interior of the Tap is nice, all dark wood and cool air. The place smells clean, which is unusual. Customers can be messy, and employees don't like scrub buckets. I wave at the bartender—we used to work together at another bar—and grab the third stool at the table next to Bobby's new girl.

"This is Crystal," Bobby says without looking up.

"Hello, Crystal."

"Hi. I've heard a lot about you."

"Good stuff, I hope."

And this is where the conversation veers off course, courtesy of Bobby.

"I haven't said shit about you," Bobby says.

Crystal squints, looking at me and then Bobby, trying to figure out if he's serious.

"Well, if you'd talked about me, you'd have said nice things."

"Not necessarily." Bobby's thin brown hair is plastered to his forehead. He's drinking shots, and he has three lined up. He sucks one in like he's taking a breath.

"Pleased to meet you, Crystal," I say.

She nods. She has a pleasant face and large breasts. The latter would explain Bobby's attention. She turns on her stool to face me. "You're Mark, right?"

"Call me Slag. If Bobbie told you anything, it's that I don't like my first name."

"Slag," she repeats.

"If fits him," Bobby says.

She frowns, turning her forehead to corduroy. "I don't think so."

"You don't get paid to think."

"I don't get *paid* at all," she says with a smirk.

Bobby was a coworker before he was a friend. I tended bar. He waited tables. The restaurant industry refers to waiters as *trons*—short for *wait-trons*—a fine, gender-neutral term hinting at a robotic inability to think. Trons irritate bartenders by forgetting to place a drink order and demanding it on the fly. Or placing the wrong drink order and acting like someone else made the mistake. Bobby never did. One night, he got into a brawl with the night manager, and that was it for him at that establishment.

He bounced around town, waiting tables someplace new until, inevitably, he got fired again. But I kept running into him. People in the restaurant industry drink. I'd go out for a few, and there he was, his big, round face grinning at me, buying me a drink. Fun to listen to him run his mouth. Every time he lost a job, a good story was sure to follow. After a while, drinking with Bobby became a habit, like ordering the same sandwich from a deli.

Many of Bobby's stories were revenge-fueled. When one manager fired him for fighting, Bobby went to the guy's home and sealed every keyhole he could find with liquid cement. Sealed his car doors, too. When the car alarm went off, Bobby smashed a window before running away. Halfway down the block, he became angry with himself for running and doubled back to bust both headlights.

Understand that Bobby tells these stories over shots. Are they true? Can't say for sure. But my guess is that some of them probably happened because I've seen the *bad smile*. Not the little-boy grin he gives to men he likes and women he's trying to con. The smile he wears when his eyes go dark, like he's Jack Nicholson, or maybe Jack's bastard lovechild, Christian Slater. It's all in the eyebrows. What comes next is a brawl.

I was on the receiving end of that look once. I'd gone to one of the bars on Basswood Street. Bobby was there, talking loud and being more Bobby-like than usual. He'd broken up with his latest girl and wanted to share a few bedroom stories. I wasn't in the mood to listen and told him so. I don't know how much he'd had to drink, but it had to be a lot because he gave me the bad smile and hit me on the side of the head.

His switch flipped just that quick.

I shook it off. Bobby could hold his own, but right then, he was drunk and wobbly. While we stood there looking at each other, the bartender came running up, shouting, "You both gotta go!" I reached for my wallet, but he shook me off. "No, no, you gotta go. Now! And don't come back here for a while." So, we went.

Outside, I told Bobby, "If you're going to sucker punch somebody, you need to make sure they go down. Otherwise, someone will fuck you up real bad."

"Who?" he asked. "You?"

"Not me," I said. "Not tonight." And I went home.

That's how Bobby ended up at my apartment the one and only time he ever visited. I didn't think he knew where I lived, but he knocked on the door three hours after he punched me, wearing the little-boy smile, carrying a bottle of rosé as a peace offering. "My Mom serves this shit at Christmas and on Columbus Day, so I figure it's classy and all." I warned him about

Sasha and went to put the bottle in the tiny fridge in the half-room. When I returned carrying a pint of Maker's Mark, he was sitting at my desk, making a fuss over my dog.

After a while, he said, "Sorry, man."

And that was that.

Sometimes Bobby will disappear for a month or two. He won't show on a Friday because he's back in county lockup, mostly for assault. He admits his mistakes, though he once angrily denied a domestic violence beef. I believed his side of the story. His devout Catholic mother would beat him senseless if he ever laid a hand on a woman.

Crystal asks me what I do for a living, which brings me back to the Tap-and-Wing. The beer in front of me is half gone. Don't remember drinking it.

"He's a private investigator," Bobby says.

I correct him. "Private security."

"Really? Do you carry a gun?" She glances down around my hip, and Bobby notices.

"Only the one God gave him," Bobby said. "Slag doesn't need a weapon. He's a boxer."

"You box?" she asks. Her lip curls up a little, like boxing is the sporting equivalent of sour milk.

I shrug. "Used to. Wasn't good enough to do anything with it."

Back when I turned seventeen, I fought for the Colorado-New Mexico Golden Gloves and held my own. Had dreams of going pro, but so does everyone. Only those lucky few touched by the Gods have the speed, the power, and the stamina to win in the pro game. I had some speed, but not much else. Besides, mixed martial arts were on the rise, and boxing didn't have the same shine as back in the day. No kicking.

Don't get me wrong. I have nothing against kicking someone, especially when they're down, but I prefer the sweet science to martial arts.

"What's the difference between private security and private investigation?" Crystal asks.

"The license." Her expression shows she doesn't understand, so I explain. "Private investigation needs certification. Private security doesn't.

That's changing, of course. The government wants to regulate the security industry, same as everything else."

"I don't blame them," she says. "I keep reading about people getting shot by security people. Too many armed amateurs if you ask me."

"Which explains why I don't carry a gun."

"Hmmm. You seem like the kind of guy who would own a lot of guns."

"I own guns. I don't carry them." That brings on an awkward silence, so I try to steer the conversation to her. "So, what do you do?"

"She does me," Bobby says.

The silence and her expression tell me Bobby has crossed a line. "What the fuck, Bobby? You've been on me all night."

"I'm on you every night," Bobby says.

That's when she slaps him.

For a second, I wonder if I'm going to see the bad smile again, until I remember Bobby's mom. He wouldn't dare raise a hand to this gal. But he's already done damage with his words.

"You fucking asshole," Crystal says, then her face screws up tight and she starts to cry. She fumbles for her purse and stands. "We're done."

"Okay."

"Okay? *Okay?* Is that all you have to say to me?"

Bobby stares at her, his gaze on her face, then on her chest. "See you when the sag sets in."

A sound comes out of her, like someone being strangled. She turns away, and in a moment, she's gone.

I'm speechless, nearly. "Jesus, Bobby. That was an asshole thing to do." I pause. "There are some lines that good people don't cross, you know?"

"We were about done anyway," he says, wiping his mouth with his sleeve. "We've been arguing a lot. Why drag things out?" He downs his last shot. I half expect him to toss the glass across the room, but he sets it gently on the table. Then, slowly, he looks up at me. "Sorry I said those things with you here."

"I'm not the one you should apologize to."

He snorts. "Let me ask you, Slag. Did you think she was the one? The one for me?"

"No. I'm not sure there is such a person."

He leans forward. "You don't believe in romantic shit any more than I do. You whine about it every time you get drunk. So, in a way, I was doing her a favor."

"There are smarter ways to end a relationship."

"You're wrong. I'm going to tell you a secret. Every woman I dump is better off. And I don't drag things out. I don't make them second guess shit. Besides, I gave her something to bitch about. She'll tell that story 200 times before she's through. That story will be worth more to her than I ever was."

"Now that you've explained it, I see what a hero you are."

Billotte's face is a mask. I hope he doesn't do something he's going to want to apologize for three hours later.

"You're right," he says finally. "I'm an asshole." Then, he smiles. "I'm getting another shot. Beer for you?" The thought of another round seems to have cheered him.

I shake my head. "I don't get it. I'm not judging you. I'm just curious, because you don't' seem very upset."

"Well, I am kind of sad about things," he says. "I'll probably get her name tattooed on my ass tomorrow." Then he pounds the table, making the empty glasses jump. "Not," he laughs, as if he's just told the best joke in history.

Chapter Three
Lloyd Stays Upright

"There are some people that just attract violence to them. No matter where they go, they'll find a fight."
~Antony Starr

You lose momentum when you double back and explain things, particularly when the story is full of strange twists and murky motivations. But you might be wondering why I'm friends with a guy like Bobby Billotte. He's an asshole with a volatile temper. He uses women. He likes Sasha, but even Hitler liked dogs.

So what? I know what I know.

The night my marriage ended, I went straight to a nightspot that catered to college students. Dark place full of black lights, fluorescent paint, and more people than the health code permits. I pushed my way through the crowd and wedged myself closer to the bar. In a place like that, the bartenders are kids pouring shots. They don't know Mr. Boston, and they don't give a damn about service. Pour a drink, grab a tip. Maybe wipe the spills on the bar top at the end of the shift. Maybe not.

I waited on the kid in the white shirt for a drink, while he waited on girls and ignored me. The black lights turned his shirt neon purple. When the fourth girl in line stepped up, overweight and pierced like a pin cushion, he turned to me. I bought three shots of top shelf whiskey, though I didn't really come for the alcohol.

There are two kinds of barfights. The sloppy ones happen when two guys go crossways over too many drinks. Hurt feelings are more likely than hurt body parts. The other kind of fight is no accident. Some people like trouble, and those crazies look for the bouncers. Bouncers are fight magnets. If I ever own a bar, I'll fire all the bouncers and hire women as bartenders. Even the college punks are reluctant to hit a woman. Besides, there are some tough-assed women out there who can keep assholes in line.

As for me, I was looking for a bouncer.

Shots in hand, I found a corner and began to drink. The first shot went down hot, landing like a grenade in my stomach. The impact left me shaking and sour, which is to say that my stomach and my head were properly aligned. That's when I spotted Tre Jensen. I saw his big head floating over the sea of drinkers, a foot above the crowd. I downed a second shot. Tre had a swatch of red hair, cut short but unruly just the same. Wherever he walked, the crowd parted, like he was Moses.

Tre Jensen was the bar's bouncer.

I decided three shots wasn't going to be enough. After I finished off the first three, I got in line behind six college girls and watched the purple bartender give away free drinks. He charged me, of course. Two more shots.

Back in my corner, I watched Tre. Arms like the pistons on a power shovel. He didn't turn like a person—the top half of his body swiveled, and his legs followed suit. He was looking at me. A pro knows in advance where the trouble's going to come from. Tre was a pro.

I downed my fourth shot. I was feeling woozy. The hurt wasn't gone—it would take years to feel like she didn't matter anymore—but the alcohol had spread the pain around evenly and wrapped it in gauze. What remained was the need to punch someone. The local boxing club had closed forever, and the nearest ring was in Denver, sixty miles away. This would have to do.

Tre was busy hard-eying me. I wanted to take my last shot of whiskey before throwing down. As Tre started across the room, I stood and squared up. Part of me craved the beating coming my way. Boxers don't just love to hit—they love being hit, too. It satisfies some inner need. And in a world gone crazy, one of us was about to impose control.

I downed the last drop just as Tre arrived. He pointed at the empty shot glass and said, "That's it. You're through for the night."

I smiled into his chest. Tre was a big boy.

"You got something to say?" he asked.

I felt myself slammed back against the wall, and my field of vision went Dutch angle. Bobby Billotte had inserted himself between us and was talking fast to Tre.

"He's my friend. I'm taking him home, okay?"

Tre shook his head. "He's out of control."

"I know, I know. That's why I'm getting him out of here. You won't have any trouble from us. Let me take him out, Tre. We won't come back. I promise."

By now, I'd righted myself. I tried to speak, but my mouth was all gum and sandpaper.

"Come on," Bobby said, dragging me sideways. I tried to resist, but by then, my efforts were focused on staying upright. Bobby pulled me through the crowd and out the door. The fresh air hit my lungs, and my head began to hurt.

"What the hell?" he asked.

I told him what had happened.

"I live four blocks from here," he said. "Can you make it?"

I did, though I stopped halfway to puke.

Bobby's place was a ground-floor studio apartment. He had me take off my shoes, then shoved me onto his bed. He fetched a towel from the bathroom and pitched it at me. "If you're going to puke again, do it in the towel. Don't throw up on my bedspread."

He spent the night on the easy chair in the corner.

The next morning, I apologized. "You did a nice thing for me with Tre," I told him. "I didn't know you could be so diplomatic."

Bobby shook his head. "You weren't acting like yourself. I had to act like you." He paused. "I gotta tell you—being reasonable is too much fucking work. I don't like it."

So, yeah. Bobby Billotte is an asshole. He's also my friend.

* * * * *

I spend Saturday morning in the park with Sasha. We could walk there—the park is close to home—but I drive anyway. No other cars around, and I have my pick of parking spots. Sasha begins to whine in anticipation. I open the door, and she bounds past the kiddie train and the playground in a joyful burst of energy. Experts call that kind of run the "fraps," which stands for frenetic random activity periods. I follow her with a string of poop bags and a muffin from the bakery in Old Town Square. It's gluten-free, because the few normal muffins they make are sold out by the time I arrived. Mine tastes like raisins and cardboard, and Sasha finishes the second half for me. We're a team.

The sky is Colorado blue, a deep, cloudless color, midway between azure and sapphire. The sun feels good on my face.

Behind us, City Park Lake slumbers, smelling of algae and goose droppings. Ahead, the playground is roped off with orange plastic tape to make sure no one tries to use the swings and slides—a reminder of the last time the city shut down the playgrounds and churches. No one's bothered to remove the tape, so people continue to follow the CDC guidelines.

The town has leash laws. I trained Sasha to carry her leash in her mouth, and though she's running like she's possessed, they'll have a tough time ticketing me.

As early as it is, there aren't many families out. If I see children, I'll have to take Sasha back to the car. Kids don't know how to act around dogs, and parents don't have sense enough to keep their kids away. I don't need animal control coming around because some brat thought it was a good idea to go nose-to-nose with my girl.

Watching Sasha run, I plan the rest of my day, beginning with background checks for people on Kelly Mason's list. First up will be Maurice Brown, a restauranteur who's having a high-profile battle with Health and Environment over health code violations. Others on the "list of enemies" include Armando de San Martín, a City Council member, head of the Community Center and advocate for Latino issues. He went after Walter last year for staffing Health and Environment without a single person of

Latin descent, a conflict that kept the local news focused on community hiring for more than a month. The third person on the list is a professor at the college. Linderman. A conflict-of-interest accusation is involved—something to do with acquiring research equipment from a company in which Walter Mason has a financial interest. Finally, Walter has a subordinate—Naomi Adriana. She probably wants his job.

When those searches are out of the way, I'll investigate Ms. Kelly Mason herself. At least that part of the job will be enjoyable.

Opening a case with background checks is standard procedure. At our first interview, I warned Kelly I'd be researching her, her husband, and the names on her list, and my search would be expensive. Inquiries of a certain type cost by the piece, anywhere from fifteen bucks a pop to ninety, depending on the service. The markup at my end can be steep. I'll decide what to actually charge her when the final bill is tallied.

Sasha is still running. Makes me wonder how she stays cooped up in my room-and-a-half without going crazy.

At the first sight of a family—Mom, Dad and a plump little thumb sucker—I call for her, and she comes to me, leash in mouth. She's worked up a good lather. I'll take her home, feed her, and get myself to work.

Whatever I don't finish in the afternoon will have to wait. Tonight, I tend bar.

* * * * *

I serve drinks at Wesley's, a modest steakhouse at the north end of Old Town. They specialize in high-end prime cuts, seasoned and seared in brass pans and finished in a wood-fired oven. The clientele likes their top shelf liquor. Manhattan with a twist. Rob Roy. Irish Mist. Old Fashioned. You know, vintage drinks. I sell some beers, too, but only craft microbrews.

Wesley's tries for a rustic look, with a lot of oak and old-time décor. But the bar top is granite, and some of the tables are aluminum. There's an ornate chandelier in the rear, where the ceiling is elevated. Colored track lighting behind the bar. Some restaurants need an interior designer.

The owner is a former cook who wanted to specialize in New York Strips and name the place The Strip Club. In the end, common sense prevailed, and he gave the restaurant his older brother's name. There's a plaque for big brother on the wall in back. Fighter pilot, died in Iraq.

Warren, the owner, got his parent's recessive genes. Short and stout, hairy arms and a bald head. He's halfway in the bag most nights, but he stays in the kitchen during the shift, so the place maintains a classy reputation.

Saturday night is the best shift of the week for a bartender. Great tips. Normally, a one-shift-a-week guy would have no shot working a Saturday, but I've been working at Wesley's since it opened, and I'm known for being able to spot trouble and head it off before something bad happens. Most of the time, this means quieting down a table of drunk college students. Occasionally, thugs come around, and Warren's glad to have me.

Bartending isn't easy. Wesley's is too small an operation to have a barback, which means I do my own keg-hauling. I set the bar up alone and tear it down at the end of the night. I'm on my feet for nine hours, never really standing still, and I must be nice to people.

But I don't mind bartending. Like Sasha, I need to get out once a week. The hard work is welcome. Putting on black and whites is a little like wearing a leash, but I look good in a vest, so there's that.

Later, when the shift winds down and the kitchen closes, the service industry folk roll in with cash in their pockets and good intentions toward a bartender who knows how to pour heavy. Warren likes to hang out in his office and count the cash over beers, which allows me to keep serving customers until after midnight.

The last hour is the best hour of the night. Waiters and cooks talk, and I listen. I hear all the stories about problem customers, asshole managers, and insane owners. I learn which businesses are thriving, and which ones are bouncing checks to the staff. I hear all kinds of rumors about other things as well, and a surprising number of them turn out to be true.

It's called networking.

Tonight, my pal Lloyd Robinson comes in after his cook shift. We used to work together at a place south of here. He's a small, slender man with an occasional mustache and the facial bumps some black men get from shaving.

His hair is beginning to thin, so he keeps it cut close, like a stubble scalp is his choice, not nature's. Lloyd is an alcoholic who drinks shots, mostly vodka. He thinks no one can smell the alcohol on him. He's certainly not fooling anyone—he gets stumbling drunk after just a few sips.

I pour him a shot of the new local distillery's product. I tell him it's on me. "I want your opinion," I say. Lloyd works at Downtown Chicken, and I'm not lying. I want his opinion. But not about the vodka.

Lloyd shoots the drink, then sits back, licking his lips as if to get a taste of what he just knocked back without tasting. "That's pretty smooth."

"That's what I thought." I pour him another. "Busy tonight?"

Lloyd shrugs. "Not really. Not like it used to be." He does to the second drink what he did to the first. "Really smooth. I like this."

"I'll tell the boss," I say. "Speaking of bosses, how's yours doing? Downtown Brown?"

Lloyd shakes his head. "Downtown Mo-licious Brown," he laughs. "The man is crazy."

I step to the left and serve a couple of gals from the pub south of us. They're wearing their work clothes—little black dresses—and they're already lit. I make their Cosmos and head back to Lloyd, pouring him a third shot. He squints at me. "I don't have a lot of money," he says. "Rent's due."

"You're drinking free," I tell him. "Product testing."

"Well, all right!" he says, the shot glass already in his hand, headed for his mouth.

"So, I heard your boss is battling with the health department." I'm pressing a little, but my window of opportunity is small. More trons and cooks are coming in, and in a minute, Lloyd is going to fall off his stool.

"You heard right," he says. "You know he's crazy, right? Did I ever tell you about the time he faced down a table of bikers?"

A dozen times. Three bikers came to town, presumably looking for a place to fight. On the way, they stopped in for chicken and shots, and proceeded to make a nuisance of themselves. Mo Brown visited the table and quieted them. In the retelling, the story acquired important symbolic details, like the American flag sewed to the biggest biker's vest, and the injudicious use of the "n" word. Best of all was Mo gripping the biker's face with a

Vulcan mind-meld, a move Lloyd was able to describe in detail. "Afterward, the bikers just sat there pouting. Then they left," Lloyd finishes.

"So, what about the health department?" I pour a fourth shot, which is as far as I'm going to go. I have limits.

"You know they've shut us down? Twice! This week, they came out again, standing around with clipboards and tape measures. Then, they all go into Mo's office, which isn't big enough for him, let alone him and two inspectors. After a while, I hear some shouting, and Mo comes out all angry and shit. The inspectors run out the back door, and Mo looks at me and says, *I'm going to kill that motherfucker.* And it's Mo, right? When he says someone's going to die, I believe him."

"He threatened to kill the inspector?"

Lloyd blinks. "No, I don't think so."

"I thought you just said—"

"The health inspectors were women. And there were two of them. He didn't say, *I'm going to kill those bitches.* But someone's in trouble, that's for sure. And I wouldn't want to be that someone." He downs the shot. He's beginning to sway on the barstool. At the door, Glen from the brewpub across the street comes in with his waitress girlfriend. I can never remember her name. I think of her as Glenda. Glen and Glenda. The names fit, since they're both blond, skinny, and perfect. Like tennis partners. Like the husband and wife in a toothpaste ad. I look at Lloyd and frown. "You got a ride home tonight?"

"I'm all right," he says.

'No, you're not. You just had four shots in about ten minutes. You aren't driving, are you?"

"Oh, hell no. I lost my license in January. I'm walking home."

I tap the bar with my knuckles. "Good. I don't want you to kill yourself behind the wheel."

"That," he says, trying hard to enunciate, "would be a tragedy."

Chapter Four
Two of Me

"Some men are just very good at cheating and lying."
~Coleen Nolan

When I think about the last time I saw my ex-wife, I pair the memory with one from our wedding. Young bride, lace dress, with a shy smile. Deep brown eyes, open wide, as if glimpsing a bright future. A sweet, nervous laugh. I remember that woman, but see her from a distance, as if watching her from across the street. Across a decade. The second memory? The closeup? That was two years ago, in our bed. And she wasn't alone.

It's natural that cases of infidelity make my stomach queasy.

I'm sitting across the street from the municipal building at seven o'clock. It's late summer, threatening to become early fall. There are wildfires fifty miles to the west. The sun throws red, smoky light across the parking lot. A person might enjoy the view if not stuck watching Walter's car.

Earlier in the day, I located Walter's Escalade, courtesy of the license plate number and work address on Kelly's fact sheet. I backed into a parking spot, far enough away for caution and close enough to keep tabs. Then me, my pee bottle and my sandwich settled in for a wait. Can't keep the car's AC running—Betsy's cooling system leaks. Instead, the windows are down. Tom Petty's playing on Betsy's dashboard cassette player.

Betsy is old school.

Just as *Last Dance with Mary Jane* cycles past for the third time, Walter comes out of the back entrance of the building. He stops by the driver's side door of the Escalade and looks around, like a groundhog searching out winter. Then he ducks inside and starts the car.

Turning Betsy's key, I put her in drive, but Walter is backing out slow, like a student driver. I suck in a breath and grip the wheel, waiting. When he leaves the lot, he crawls. I fantasize about ramming him from behind, but my poor car would fold like origami on Walter's rear bumper. He turns right out of the parking lot and heads two blocks to a red light. From there, he turns left and pulls into one of the parking spots in the median.

Two blocks. He drove two blocks.

I wait at the light long enough to see him head into a restaurant on Main Street. I know the pace. They serve fresh fish (or what passes for fresh in a landlocked state). I circle the block six times until a parking space opens up with a view of both Walter's car and the front windows of the fish house. The interior of the restaurant is well-lit, so I can see Walter. He's sitting with four other people. Three men and a woman. I need to pee—the orange juice bottle—wide mouth for a reason—comes into play. Peeing in public always makes me nervous. A passerby could glance in and take me for a pervert. Perverts are frowned upon.

On the seat beside me sits my cellphone with its excellent camera, inserted inside an adapter mount, outfitted with a monocular spotting scope. More importantly, I still have half a sandwich left and two unopened cans of Red Bull.

Inside, Walter divides his attention equally, paying no special attention to the woman. She's a brunette, tastefully dressed in a navy-blue business suit. Short bobbed hair. Pretty, from what I can see, but nothing terribly special. I may be dead ending here. Nevertheless, I'm on the clock, and due diligence rules the day.

Kelly Mason hired me to find out who was threatening her husband. Most times, the threat starts with a sin. No lever—no leverage. This man has everything. Nice clothes. A good job. A beautiful wife. A car with a cooling system. But he's cheating. *I know it.* And finding out what he's being threatened with is the first step—the most important step—in finding out who's after him.

Investigators are lazy. They don't mind racking up billable hours any more than a lawyer does, but covering every possible base is a pain in the ass, especially in a one-man operation. I have a feeling about this, and I'm going to follow my instincts. Their dinner won't last forever, and I have nothing else planned.

Watching people eat makes me hungry. I unwrap the second half of my sub sandwich—a cold cut combo without tomatoes so the leftovers don't get soggy. Inside, Walter is chuckling, a tight smile on his face. Never an open-mouthed laugh. When he eats, he slips tiny forkfuls through barely parted lips. Little bites, mincing steps. Walter sips at the world like it's his own personal wine glass.

I snap two photos for reference. My sandwich is gone fifteen minutes before Walter cleans his plate.

Why would someone cheat on Kelly Mason? Tight body, beautiful face. What's not to love? For the tenth time, I list the possibilities. Is she cold? Demanding? Is she a shrew? She's certainly not slow-witted—our interview told me that much. More likely, the fault lies with Walter. Here's a simple truth you can take to the bank—men who have everything want more.

Walter makes a show of paying the tab while the group sits chatting. For the wait-tron's sake, I hope he's a good tipper. Somehow, I doubt it. Walter likely pays with a county credit card or an expense account, and there are probably regulations about how much government people can tip. There are regulations for everything.

When the group stands to leave, two of the men bow and exit, leaving Walter, the brunette, and one other man—a stout fellow with a tight top button, a red face, and a bolo tie. His neck spills over his collar in folds. Just looking at him makes me want to mop sweat from my forehead. Finally, they all stand and head for the door.

I fire Betsy up and wait.

The three leave the restaurant together, pausing outside the front door. At the light, the man turns left. There's a parking garage farther down the street. Walter and the woman wave goodbye, wait a moment, then head the opposite way up Main Street, passing the restaurant again. He's being a gentleman, walking her to her car.

The sidewalks are busy, full of young people. Some of them are carrying signs. Walter and the woman navigate the crowd. Halfway up the block, in plain sight, she slips her hand into his.

Bingo.

She's parked at the end of the street. She'll back up and head south, so I wait for her to pass me. They talk for a moment—no kiss—then part ways. As predicted, she drives south. I swing out behind her.

Here's something worth knowing. If you want to shake someone tailing you, the first thing you do is let them know that you know you're being followed. With their cover blown, a lot of guys will back off. If not, look for a big rig or something that will block the view, use it to your advantage. If you're in a turn lane, waiting out a light, shoot the gap—turn before you get the green arrow. Of course, none of that's in play if you don't know you're being followed. And though Walter might glance around before he steps into his car, his brunette doesn't suspect a thing.

She drives her Prius to the other side of town, turning west at the southern tip of Westbrook. From there, she drives straight toward the mountains. She's got a heavy pedal foot. I push Betsy to keep up. Halfway to the foothills, she runs a red and I'm stuck waiting. She's no more than a block ahead when I decide to run the same light. If I get pulled over, so be it. I'll bill the ticket to Kelly Mason and her husband.

Luckily, I haven't lost her. She's still moving due west. When she finally turns left, she enters a subdivision with huge, expensive homes. Family homes. Though predictable, this is a mild disappointment. I'd hoped Ms. Brunette would live in an apartment house. I would be done following Walter—you don't need to chase the bee when you know where the hive is. But she won't bring Walter here. She pulls into her driveway, parking next to a white Subaru.

Ms. Brunette is married.

I pass by slow enough to catch the address, then drive on. It takes five or ten minutes to weave my way back to the main road. Nice houses with manicured lawns and hybrid cars in the driveways, but no sense at all when it comes to laying out the side streets.

Rich people.

The rest of the night is mine. I drive Betsy back to my reserved parking spot in the alley behind my building. The heavens open and rain down their blessings—no car has taken my spot. It's a Monday night. On a Saturday, a student would have parked their parent's car in my spot by now, and I'd have to park down the street and move Betsy back again in the morning.

There's a lot of noise in Old Town Square tonight. I hear it as soon as I step out into the alley. As I wind my way past the alley dumpsters, heading for the square, I step into a floodlit slice of Armageddon. Chanting. People climbing the fountain, brandishing signs. A female in a hoodie runs past me from the right, throwing a shoulder as she passes. I hear breaking glass. There are no guards in front of the stores. The trash can by the bike rack is on fire. Across the way, I see people on the rooftop of the bar Billotte likes, looking down on the cacophony.

I walk a half block along the storefronts, past the mostly gluten-free bakery, my head on a swivel. Someone is whacking the piano with a collapsible wand. Ahead, a young man—perhaps a student—is blocking my path. He's wearing dark clothes, but then, so am I. He points at his sign. I nod. He nods back and lets me by.

I'm wary about passing him. When the crowd's fury is up, people get sucker punched. Blindsided. No rules—the Marquis of Queensbury is just another old, dead white man. But the young man's nod seems genuine, and I have no choice. I want to go home. My eyes are fixed on the door ahead, shoulders hunched against a blow that doesn't come.

Then I'm inside. I go up the stairs to the bathroom at the end of the hall, anxious to pee somewhere besides inside a bottle. I should take Sasha for a walk but taking her outside now seems sketchy. Perhaps people will get tired and go home in an hour or two so she can empty her bladder.

Inside the apartment, Sasha is nervous, like she always is when the crazies come out to play. I stand at the window, parting the blinds and looking down. Someone sees me, silhouetted by the light. He gives me a middle-finger salute.

I wonder who cranked their keys, these little windup toys. I suppose I could grab the local news-pamphlet and read about the latest atrocities, but that would be a form of self-flagellation.

At my first bartending job, I worked with a guy from Eastern Europe. He liked to complain about the United States, and after a while, it rankled me. We can't play soccer. We all act like we're cowboys. A sophisticated person can't find *Štrukli* in our crappy American bakeries.

One day, we argued about journalism, and I expressed the opinion that journalism doesn't exist where he came from—just a series of harvest reports. Grain. Corn. Cattle. And none of the numbers were true. He didn't blink. "And your news? Murders. All you report is the murder harvest."

Easter Europe defeats USA, 1-zip.

Now, my town prints a single sheet of paper, folds it into quarters like a greeting card, stuffs it with ads and sells it for four dollars. Nothing in the way of local news, God forbid. Only wire service recaps. All bullshit. A decade ago, I gave a damn.

I pour myself a glass of whiskey, turn out the lights, pull a chair to the window to watch. Better than television. Sasha pads over and hunkers next to my chair, her head on her paws. The damage below seems less drastic than with some previous kerfuffles, and the crowd is half as large as the one after the last election. Tomorrow, the city will send out sweepers and power-washers. The shop owners will call glass companies. The square will be clean and ready for families by the weekend. Everything will be calliope music and popcorn again.

Unless this is the start of another anger jag. Then, all bets are off.

This is the new world. Like snowstorms in Minnesota—after a while, snow doesn't mean as much. You get used to the plows.

I raise the rocks glass to my lips and find it empty. Surprised, I glance down at Sasha. "Are you drinking my whiskey?" I ask. She doesn't even look up. She's used to my accusations.

I refill the glass, my eyes locked on the plaza. They're singing something now, a song I don't recognize. Not that I would—I stopped listening to new music a decade ago. The singing is disjointed, like people fumbling through Happy Birthday at a party.

I take another sip. "Here's to you all," I whisper.

I secretly envy them. They believe in something. They don their black clothing and make a joyful noise unto their whatever, like ninja Pentecostals. Their Gods are beards and berets on blood red tee-shirts—as empty and vacant as the myth of the grandfather God. But rather than kneel, they burn things. Good. The world needs a little fire.

But not my apartment. I worry for my dog.

I wonder how old Sasha is. Six? Ten? The vet doesn't know. She's a big girl, and it's hard to tell. How many years do we have left together? I look down at her mournfully. She looks up this time, a pained look on her face. I know the look.

She has to pee.

I stand up, and she jumps to attention. When I grab the leash, she begins to whimper with anticipation. I need to pee again, too, and I just went. How is she holding it in?

We go down the stairs, the leash gripped tight. If we're going out into the Battle Royale, I want to be able to rein her in.

I open the door slowly. She can't growl, but the fur on her back is standing up. I pull her to the right, heading for the alley. I just want to let her do her business and get back home. The young man in black is gone, but a trio of women stand in his place, blocking me. One of them seems charmed by Sasha and rushes forward to pet her. She should ask. Like a child, the woman drops down and grabs Sasha by the muzzle.

When Sasha bares her teeth, I pull her back. "Sorry," I say. "She's a rescue dog. She's not comfortable with people."

The girl is rail-thin, wearing torn jeans and sandals. Fall nights are cold in Westbrook, and I wonder if her feet are cold.

"It's okay, I'm a dog person," she explains, moving forward again, hands outstretched. The other two women are scowling at me. I'm older than they are, and I'm not wearing sandals. I'm probably the enemy.

Sasha snaps, and the girl jumps back, shocked.

"I'm so sorry—"

The girl crosses her arms in front of her chest. She seems both horrified and betrayed.

"He probably abuses her," a short, squat woman offers. "Look at the dog's ear." Her shrill voice carries judgement like ice water in a bucket.

"She has to pee," I say, swinging past them, headed for the alley.

On the way, I see that the bakery's window is cracked—the spider web of lines spans four feet. One good poke will send the glass tumbling. I think of the woman who waits on me in the morning three times a week. Ana? Alma? Will the bakery open tomorrow, or will they send her home while repairs are being made? Will she miss the money? I picture her square face and small, pursed mouth, and I imagine her asking a landlord for a deferral on her rent.

Adella. Her name is Adella.

In the alley, Sasha squats and pees a river while I wait. Only fair—she certainly waited for me. When she's finished, I steer back to the mouth of the alley, anxious to get home. Ahead, the girl in sandals is waiting. Alone.

"I'm sorry," she says.

"It's okay. No harm done, right?"

I try to swing around her, but the girl steps to the side, blocking me. Her arms are still crossed in front of her chest, and she's shivering. "My friend is an asshole. She shouldn't have said that."

It takes me a moment to figure out who she's talking about.

"I don't think you mistreat your dog. You clearly care for her."

I nod. Maybe she *is* a dog person.

"I'm Shelly," she says.

"Call me Slag."

She seems confused. "Is that short for something?"

"Short for Slag." I laugh.

"A nickname, then."

I nod. "Well, Shelly," I say. "It was nice chatting with you."

"You should be out here with us, you know," she says.

I watch as someone short, dressed in black and a ski mask, runs past us like the hounds of hell are chasing him. I glance behind me, tracking him down the alley, his path illuminated by cones of light staged at intervals, dumpster by dumpster. The night air is crisp and cool, and there's a hint of moisture in the air. I turn back and stare at Shelly. She appears to be waiting for an answer.

I shrug.

"Really. What we're doing is important."

"I suppose it is," I say. "But it's your thing. It's not my thing."

"Everyone has to be part of it. You can't just tread water, you know. You have to swim."

This catches me off guard. I stare, as if I've had my cards read. Treading water? The story of my life. Her expression is painfully sincere. Open, vulnerable eyes. An upturned nose, resting on her face like an exclamation point.

"I'm glad you have a cause," I say, speaking carefully. "I do, too. I want my dog to be able to piss."

Chapter Five
Minnie

"The most mediocre of males feels himself a demigod as compared with women."
~Simone de Beauvoir

I spend two days tracing various elements of the case. Kelly Mason is going to be upset when she finds out what her husband is doing. She'll likely turn her anger in my direction. She hired me to find out who is blackmailing Walter, not find out if he's a cheat. I need to tell her something she asked to know. So, I research her enemies list.

When you investigate someone, you start on the outside and work your way in. Talk to people who know your subject from a distance. Then, move closer. Talk to employees or coworkers. Family, especially if they're estranged.

Any information you discover will help you when you go face-to-face. I'll have to talk to Walter eventually. An unscrupulous investigator might use incriminating evidence for a side hustle. *Your wife doesn't have to see this. We can make it go away.* But that's not me.

Walter's interview will go like any other. Start off with casual questions. Friendly. Dish a little of your own information to build some trust. Don't be an asshole. And above all, *listen.* If your target is talking, shut up and let him (or her) talk.

Ask open-ended questions. Never show your hand. The information you gather is for follow-up questions. To use a boxing metaphor, your information makes a good counterpunch. That's not to say you ask leading questions, hoping for a gotcha. That undercuts trust. But when interviewing, your goal is to get at the truth. That takes work.

Meanwhile, your subject may be interested in obscuring the truth—and rightly so. Most *everyone* has something to hide. Walter certainly does.

You have to be clever and not tell the truth about yourself. You're a census worker. A new employee or applicant who's curious about the business. A social media consultant looking for input.

That's why it's a little risky to take a case close to home. You can get your head bashed in, and not just by husbands who've been outed. But I don't do a lot of real investigation, so I'm not worried. After all, my usual gig is security.

So, I've been busy. Out and about. Then I come home to find my next client sitting on the floor outside my door. I am surprised. Chagrined.

"Are you waiting for me?" I ask.

A nod.

"I am *so* sorry to keep you waiting."

I'm trying to figure out if my client is male or female. The earrings don't mean anything, nor does the flat chest or diminutive stature. Puffy lips, and frizzy, close-cropped hair are no help.

"Have you been waiting here a long time?"

A headshake. I'd hoped for a yes or no. Voice could give me a hint."Thank you for waiting." I stick a key in the door. "Come on in." I gesture toward my client chairs. "What's your name?"

"Minnie." Her voice is small and sweet. By now, I've used my investigative powers to ascertain that Minnie is she, though I'm not sure that's her chosen pronoun.

Minnie selects the chair on the left. I go behind the desk and grab a pen. When Minnie sits, her feet do not touch the floor. She is well-named.

Her face is angular and fragile. Not pretty, but weighty somehow. Maybe it's her eyes. Dark. Serious. *Wounded.*

"So, Minnie, how is it you came here?"

"I'm on foot."

"Ah. Great. So, how did you choose my services?"

She may be blushing. Hard to say—her skin is very dark. "Billotte sent me. He said you were friends. He said you'd fix things for free. I don't have no damned money."

I make a mental note to thank Bobby for finding pro bono work for me. Mustering a smile, I say, "Tell me what you have in mind, and I'll tell you if I can help."

Minnie, as yet without a last name, explains that she lives in a one-bedroom apartment, two blocks to the west side of Main Street. Five blocks north of Old Town. Cheap apartments and small, box-shaped houses that haven't been painted in decades. Dead lawns and broken fences. Everyone has a dog, and the dogs are mean.

"Someone needs to tell Santiago to leave me alone. He keeps threatening me, and I'm afraid he's going to . . ." Her voice trails off.

"Does Santiago have a last name?"

"Alvarez." Minnie closes her eyes.

"What makes you think he's going to hurt you?"

She opens her eyes again, scowling. "That ain't it," she says. "He doesn't scare me. Ain't no man scares me." Her bravado is touching. Like a boxer, proud of being able to take a punch. The purpled skin around her eyes argues in her favor. She leans closer, whispering. "I don't want to get pregnant. Understand?"

Mystery solved. Minnie is all woman.

My pen hovers over a spiral notebook. "Is he raping you, Minnie?" Bad interview technique. I'm supposed to put her at ease, and now she's shuffling in her seat like a tweaker. Sometimes, I do the wrong thing.

"You could call it that."

Pen down. "Have you made a police report?"

Minnie laughs. The sound is hot and raw, like tar. "Are you serious?"

"Sorry," I say, picking the pen up again. "Is Santiago your husband or a boyfriend?"

"Don't know. We lived together for a while. Told the landlord we were married. Bobo said that means we common law."

"Could be," I say. Laws change so fast. "Who's Bobo?"

She blinks. "Bobo Billotte."

Bobo. I can't wait to throw the nickname in his face. I clear my throat. "Married or not, he can't do that to you. No human being should have to put up with that."

Minnie sits back, her little frame slumping. "That's right." Her lips draw the response out, as if she's said "Thasss right," like a snake uncoiling to its full length. Maybe I haven't botched the interview after all. I make a mental note to go a little slower. *Let her talk.*

There's an old joke about a guy fattening his pig for the county fair. He puts a cork in the pig's ass and feeds it, swelling it up like a balloon. At the fair, a monkey (it's a joke—don't ask for logic) jumps into the pig's pen and pulls out the cork. When authorities arrive to survey the carnage, traumatized witnesses say, "the last thing I remember is," followed by various tragedies. The punchline comes when a witness with a clear view says, "the last thing I remember is the poor monkey trying to put the cork back in the pig."

"Tell me a little more about Santiago," I say, and just like that, the cork is out.

Santiago Alvarez is short, shaped like a refrigerator. Mean. The youngest of six brothers and two sisters, Santiago was spoiled by his sisters and forged by his brothers, who beat him daily until he could stop them from doing so. "That man likes to fight," Minnie says, shaking her head. "Ain't never seen him without cuts or bruises on his knuckles."

"Does he have an income source?"

"What does that mean?"

"Does he have a job?"

"Oh, I get it. Sorry, I don't have no good vocabulary."

I smile. Most people hide when they don't understand something. Not Minnie.

Pretending you understand what you don't has two benefits. First, you won't find out what you don't know, and what you don't know is always bad. Second, you don't have to admit you don't know everything. Plato's Socrates thought wisdom was understanding that you didn't know anything at all, but I've always thought Socrates was a smug, condescending fuck. Like a PhD who tells you some questions are unanswered—but has all the answered questions tucked in his pocket.

As for Minnie, she has no problem asking questions. Points for honesty.

Santiago's money comes from unknown sources. He's had jobs, but none lasted more than two weeks. But he always has money, kept in a roll in his front pants pocket. Smaller denominations so the roll looks fatter.

In the short time they lived together, Santiago spent at least one night a week out and about, and when he returned, often at dawn, he would come with a gift or take her out to breakfast. Minnie thought of those nights out as "payday."

Things began to sour shortly after they moved in together. Money or no money, his nights out worried Minnie. If she said anything about it, he became angry. Eventually, he began to hit her. "Santi apologizes afterward, but he's always gotta add one last word 'bout how it's my fault. *If only you hadn't done whatever. Why did you have to mention such-and-such? You set me off.* I end up apologizing, just to keep the peace."

"Hope you don't blame yourself," I say. The words slip out again, without consideration, and I think she senses that. She actually smiles. Not a pretty smile, but genuine.

After one of Santiago's physical outbursts put her in urgent care, she told him to leave. He did so, telling her the breakup was a long time coming, given that she was too controlling and too homely to bear.

As Minnie relates this last, she begins to tear up. I have boxes of Kleenex ready for duty and push one her way. She takes a moment to push in the cut-out tab and struggle the first sheet out of the box. "Thank you," she says.

"Don't mention it."

I'm portraying her in an unflattering way, and that's unfair. It's hard to imagine someone with a plain face and a boy's body as attractive, but Minnie *is* attractive, though in a different way. Beyond the "I can take a punch" bluster, there's no trace of victimhood in her—the kind of hopelessness that shifts personal responsibility to blame, elevates problems into catastrophes, and leaves no room for action. No, Minnie doesn't act like a victim.

But she *is* a victim—a woman in trouble, asking for help. I resolve to help her.

"Where can I find him?"

"He hangs out at the community center a lot," she says. "He loves the place. It's like a church to him. He gets his head stuffed full of ideas and starts using words that aren't his."

This confuses me. "What do you mean?"

"He says things like *advocacy* and *awareness*. When I ask him what the hell he's talking about, he tells me I'm stupid. I may not know everything, but I know they're not *his* damned words, and I say so. Then he hits me and tells me it's my fault, and the system's fault, because everything's run by the white man." Her face pulls into a sudden rictus. "Sorry. No offence."

"None taken," I say. "This is good information." I doodle in the spiral notebook as if I'm taking notes. "Does he work for the community center?"

"I don't know. He ought to. They ought to pay him. He's there every damned day."

This last bit of information is useful. One of the people on Kelly Mason's list is Armando de San Martin, the head of the community center. I'll talk to both of them.

When I look up from my notebook, she's shifting in her chair, clearly wanting to end her visit. "What else do you need to know?"

"You said he still comes around." I'm using euphemisms. "What happens?"

Minnie shrinks into herself, like cellophane on fire. "My fault, I guess."

"I doubt that but go on."

"See, sometimes, I let him in. Shouldn't, but I'm alone, you know? *Alone.* And sometimes you need a familiar face to let you know you're still attached to the world. Other times, he just knocks, and I have to open the door. You can't not open a door. And there he is, all smiles and promises, but it's bullshit, and by then, he's already in."

I lean forward, urgency in my voice. "Listen to me. He's the bad guy. You're not. No excuses for him."

"Maybe. But that don't help matters. Once he's there, I can't stop him."

"He's a bully, and bullies back off. I'm going to weigh down on this guy like a ton of steel. You are safe now. The moment you walked in my door, you solved your problem. I mean it."

She tilts her head and frowns. "The Po-Po can't do anything."

I smile. "Bullies back off," I repeat.

She seemed to size me up. "Santi is a bad ass."

"Bully."

"We'll see," she says, her eyes narrowing.

"Anything else?" I ask.

Her expression goes flat, regarding me with those wounded eyes. She slips out of the chair, landing on her feet. Holding her chin up, she says, "If you fuck up, it'll come back on me."

"I don't ever fuck up," I promise.

Chapter Six
Sending Santiago a Message

"Reasonable people can have differences."
~Paul Martin

After Minnie's visit, I drive to the community Center, planning to talk to Armando de San Martín or Santiago Alvarez. Either or both.

The community center is a tiny recreation facility on the north end of town. Sandwiched between an auto parts store and a tattoo parlor, the center is located ten blocks north of the old one, which was repurposed as a homeless shelter and protest site a few years back. The new center is one-third the size of the old center, which was triple the size of the still-older center. When it comes to building size, everything old is new again.

The new building looks like a shoe box. A great deal was made about the sustainable practices used to construct the place. They should have practiced harder. Limited parking because the city gave space to bike racks instead of cars. The small lot is dark in the evening, in keeping with Westbrook's light pollution restrictions. As a result, the shadows provide a home for the city's drug culture, along with various urban campers, gang members, and sexual predators.

The flat roof began leaking the first winter, and moisture caused mold issues that trigger the carbon dioxide sensors, which in turn keep the HVAC system circulating spores instead of saving energy. The smell is strong enough to give the center its nickname—*The House of Wet Socks*.

Toilets that aren't flushed twice keep souvenirs. Low-flow faucets discourage showering, even handwashing.

I know all this because the center is where I go to box. There's no ring there, but the weight room has some wrestling mats in a corner. Three of us share two sets of gloves and a heavy bag. Beggars can't be choosers.

Both guys I box with are acquainted with Armando de San Martín. Manuel thinks he's a straight shooter. Lee hasn't forgiven the center's director for turning rec space into offices, so he's got nothing nice to say. "That son of a bitch would clip desktops to the urinals if it meant he could jam another six city employees into the building."

Of course, Lee would change his tune if he got one of those six jobs. Instead, he's down at the center in the middle of the day, gloves on, talking me to death while he cuffs me in the clinch. With no ring and no ropes to hang on, Lee just steps off the mat when he needs a breather. If I hit him, which I can do at will, he calls it a "cheap shot." I mostly just shuffle around and paw at him. No use hurting a friend.

Manuel is a different sort. Quiet, serious, with dark eyes and long lashes that probably drive women crazy. And he can box. He's not as fast as me, but his left hook comes out of nowhere and feels like he's carrying a roll of quarters in his glove. I'm careful with him. He could hurt me.

When Manuel was in high school, he washed dishes at one of the restaurants I worked for. Good kid who never had much to say. He talks more now, mostly to give Lee shit, which is fine by me. Lee dishes back, of course. Calls him *Manual Labor,* which is ironic, since the kid works hard. Manuel and Lee spar, of course, and Manuel never hits him as hard as he hits me, which is another clue to the boy's good heart.

I'm shuffling across the mats with Lee now, throwing soft punches and blocking shots. He has long arms, and he ought to be able to box outside. A good jab doesn't alter the stance much, so it's harder to anticipate. Not Lee's jab, though. He cocks his arm and elbow back before pulling the trigger. When he jabs, he overextends, leaning into the motion, which makes counter-punching easy. Every time he jabs like that, I tap him, hoping he'll get the idea, but after six months of sparring, I know better.

As we box, sweat runs into my eyes and down my back. I'm puffing a little. I keep my feet moving and my head bobbing, but I'm getting tired. I'm older than either of these guys by a decade. It's beginning to show. The thought gives me pause, and for a moment, I forget to pay attention. Mistake. A jab grazes my chin.

Now, I'm angry and counter with a combination. The harder of my two punches strikes Lee in the shoulder, so I probably hurt his feelings more than his body. Still, he steps back off the mat, mopping his forehead with the sleeve of his hoodie. "What was that?"

"Counterpunch."

"That's not what I mean. You're pissed off. I tapped you, man. I didn't unleash the full power of the pythons."

Uncoiling, I try to relax. Lee is an unhappy guy in his twenties, with no job and no prospects. He has a girlfriend, but I've seen her out with other guys, and he probably doesn't know. His pencil mustache looks stupid. He cuts his hair in a mullet. His life sucks, and I don't want to hurt his feelings. "What?" I ask, grinning. "Did I rub a little sand in your vagina?"

Manuel smirks. Lee points a glove at him. "Don't laugh."

I pull off my gloves. "Truth is, I'm tapped out. You guys are going to put me in an early grave."

"I'll drink a lot of water before they bury you," Lee says. "That way, I can piss on your grave."

I laugh. "My corpse will think it's the weak-assed beer you drink."

We take turns wiping down the mats with Lee's towel and tidying up the rest of the room, though the mess wasn't ours. Just before we leave, I ask if either guy knows Santiago Alvarez. Lee makes a show of thinking about it, running a thumb across his mustache and humming, but he doesn't know shit. Manuel knows something, but his lips are shut tight. He's looking off to the side, shaking his head.

Lee heads down the hall, gym bag swinging, like he has somewhere to go. Manuel taps my shoulder, so we hang back.

"Santi is a piece of shit," Manuel says, his voice low. "This something for work?"

I nod.

"You need to watch your back," he says, tapping my shoulder again.

We walk outside, and Manuel nods in the direction of a group of four Latinos standing next to the tents at the back edge of the lot. One of the four is built like a refrigerator. Short black hair. More ink than an office printer. One of the others, a slender boy in his teens, laughs and says something. The refrigerator slaps him in the chest, knocking him back a step.

I whisper my thanks to Manuel and move away from him. I'd rather we weren't standing together when Santiago spots me.

My hoodie is soaked with sweat. When a breeze slides between the buildings, I shiver and jam my hands into my pockets. The refrigerator sees me coming. He meets my gaze while the others keep jabbering. I stop ten feet away, which is polite, and ask, "Are you Santiago Alvarez?"

He doesn't answer. His hand floats in the air, one finger up, as if he'd been talking with his hands and I'd frozen him in mid-sentence. Close up, he's shorter than I expected. More of a fire hydrant than a refrigerator. Minnie is small enough to think he's big. Size is relative.

"Who is this?" the skinny boy asks.

No use offering a handshake. I smile instead. "I'm looking for Santiago Alvarez."

"You and he friends?" the fire hydrant asks.

"No, but we have a mutual friend."

"Who is that?"

"I'm guessing you aren't Santiago Alvarez," I say, still smiling. "My friend wants me to talk to Santiago." My smile is gone. "Not his homies."

"I don't know who you are—"

"This is about Minnie."

Nothing changes on his face. "Minnie? Minnie Mouse?"

I glance to the side. The skinny one is wide-eyed with recognition. I hook a thumb at the boy and say, "He seems to know her."

A flurry of Spanish follows. The skinny one has irritated everyone, and they all tell him to keep his mouth shut.

The fire hydrant turns and asks, "What do you want? Who is this friend of yours that knows Minnie?"

I turn to the others, tight-lipped. Audiences should be avoided, with good reason. One-on-one, most people are reasonable. They think. They interact. Add spectators into the mix, and everyone starts to perform instead of listening.

The fire hydrant barks more Spanish and closes the space between us, while the other three back up eight or ten steps. I'm afraid that's as much space as his crew is going to give me. At any rate, I have identified my Santiago.

"Don't misunderstand," I say. "Our mutual friend doesn't *know* Minnie. Our mutual friend *is* Minnie." This doesn't seem to sink in immediately. When the lightbulb finally goes off, I've start talking again. "I'm here to ask a favor. You've moved on to better things. That's great. But she's afraid—"

"Who the fuck do you think you are?" He steps even closer, which surprises me. I hold my ground.

"I meant no disrespect," I say, keeping my voice even. "This is not my side of town."

He won't look up, which means he's staring at my chest, given the height difference. I think about crouching down to look him in the eye, but that would surely trigger blows. Instead, I continue. "Minnie doesn't have a good life. Don't make it worse. Please stay clear. As a favor."

He rubs the tiny stubble beneath his lower lip that passes for a soul patch. "Are you fucking Minnie?" he asks.

"I said we were friends. That's what we are."

"How did you two meet?"

"I have other friends in the neighborhood." While I talk to Santiago, the skinny one circles me. "Your boy shouldn't get behind me," I say, hitching a thumb over my shoulder. "That's a bad place to be."

"Really? You a bad man?" Santiago raises one eyebrow.

"I'm just asking a favor. Leave her alone."

"What do I get?" he asks.

I lean in closer, whispering. "My wishes for your good health."

Again, he doesn't seem to get what I'm saying. I've met men like Santiago before. Always one half-step behind, covering up for his plodding nature with bluster, and sometimes, violence. Like I told Minnie—a bully.

He shrugs his shoulders, like a boxer loosening up before a bout. "I'm done with that bitch anyway," he says. Now he's smiling. Something in his expression makes my skin crawl. The upraised eyebrow? The tiny soul patch, like a fly crawled out of his mouth and perched under his lip? Maybe it's the kid behind me. I step back, bumping into him. The boy tries to lock in place, but he's carrying half my weight. I glance back as he stumbles away.

Enough. "I meant no disrespect," I say, backing away.

"Hey," Santiago calls. "Tell Minnie I'll be seeing her."

I stop in my tracks. This man is stupider than I thought, which makes him more dangerous. I'm still smiling, though I'm trying to hold my temper. "That would be a mistake. Listen, you don't know me, but folks here at the center will tell you. Ask around. They'll tell you—Slag Ferguson is a good guy to have as a friend."

"Slag?" he snorts.

"Slag Ferguson. Ask around. I'll be in your debt."

"Slag," he repeats, laughing. The others join in, repeating my name.

I turn to one of the three—not the skinny one, which would be too easy—and say, "*Cállate la boca.*" He freezes. I don't wait around. Ten steps farther away, I call back. "Slag Ferguson. Ask around."

"Fuck you, *payaso*," the skinny one calls. Santiago continues to stare, silent.

That could have gone better. I might have done something about it, but four against one is a formula for getting your ass kicked.

Rather than go back to my car, which I parked two blocks away (owing to an asphalt lot full of tents and bicycle racks), I go back inside the center. I'm going to ask to see Councilman Armando de San Martín. They'll put me off, of course, and I'll make an appointment. Meanwhile, I'll nose around and see what I can turn up.

The man at the reception desk asks me to wait for a moment. He has the desk phone in hand, juggling calls. He whispers into the receiver, then tells me, "The councilman will see you now."

I'm not ready for that.

The receptionist points down the hall. "First door on the right," he says, indicating a tiny office with an open door.

Tapping on the doorframe, I ask, "Are you busy?"

"Come," the councilman says before looking up.

I step in and stare at his desk.

A blueprint covers most of the desktop. He follows my gaze and immediately begins to roll the print up, a thin smile on his lips. His shirtsleeves are up, but otherwise, he has the trim, fitted look of an aristocrat. His dark eyes and aquiline nose, prominent at the bridge, add to the sense of gravitas. A suit jacket hangs on a hook behind the desk. The fabric drapes like somebody spent time and money hand-stitching and matching the pattern.

The office is small and unimpressive. The gray metal desk could have come from any cubicle. A photo of a woman and two children sits on the sill behind the desk. The woman is pretty, and the kids are cute in a suburban sort of way. The youngest, a girl, is wearing a ballcap. Her older brother has bowl-cut hair and is missing a front tooth. A white board, decorated with several phone numbers in blue marker, hangs on one wall. A clock sits on the opposite wall, with no Cave of the Winds logo evident. Plaques hang to the right of the desk. I see words like "award" and "honor." I turn back to the man.

"How can I be of service?" he asks, his voice precise and sonorous, as if the words spilled out of a radio. Everything about the man is impressive, rolled sleeves and plain office aside.

"Slag Ferguson," I say. I hold out a hand, and he gives it a firm grip. Plain wedding band. Long, tapered fingers.

"Slag. Interesting name."

"Thanks."

He folds his hands over the rolled blueprint and waits.

Time to dance. "I box here. We use the weight room. No room for a ring, so we box on top old wrestling mats."

Then, he surprises me. "You box with Manny, right?"

"Manny?" I blink.

"Manuel Ayala."

"Oh, Manuel. Sorry. Never thought of him as a Manny. Nobody who hits that hard should be named Manny." The councilman blinks. The corners of his mouth turn down. I glance at the photo before stumbling on. *With my luck, he probably named his son Manny.* "Yeah, I like the kid a lot. Smart. Good athlete."

"Yes. So, how may I help you?"

"Well, the boxing thing is tough without a ring. And sometimes, yoga girls take over the mats. There's even a couple of karate guys that practice in there." I remember what Lee said about rec space and decide I have a plausible lie going. "So, what's it going to take to get some dedicated space for boxing? I wouldn't mind teaching some classes if that would help. I used to box Golden Gloves."

The councilman sits back, sighing. "Alas, I'm afraid that under the present circumstances, there's not much chance."

"Can't the city do something? The city government must know this place isn't up to snuff. You'd think the health department would back you. This place is always crowded." I'm pushing, of course, and sounding false, even to me. But I'm playing out a bad hand.

Armando de San Martín tilts his head, not answering.

"Getting jammed into a small building sucks for everyone," I say. "Wish they'd spent more on the building and less on the bike racks. You're too far north for any students to bike out here anyway."

His face relaxes. "You have touched on an unfortunate truth. We are too far from the center of the community to be a community center." He pats the blueprint. "You'll be happy to know we have proposed a move to the heart of downtown."

"Really? You're going to replace the House of Wet Socks?"

He winces, then sniffs, as if my mention invokes the smell. "Ah, that name. Yes, well, we'd love to move. There are a great many hurdles to overcome, not the least of which is funding. Location is problematic as well. I would be remiss to offer you more than faint hope."

"Well." I bite the inside of my cheek, wondering what else to say.

He glances at his watch. "I wish I had better news. In the meantime, I hope you continue to use the weight room. You gentlemen do use mouthguards and headgear, don't you?"

"Mouthguards," I say. "Don't want to mess up the Chiclets."

"I would encourage you to use headgear as well. Our understanding of sports-related concussion has undergone significant changes over the last two decades." He pauses. "And if Manny hits as hard as you say, the precaution might be worth the effort."

I smile. "Appreciate your time, Councilman."

"Of course." He points. "As you can see, the door is always open."

I bow and step into the corridor. My song and dance about the health department didn't yield anything meaningful, but no matter. I have what I came for. The councilman may have had past differences with Walter Mason, but I suspect they're working together on the new community center. Meanwhile, someone else just jumped to the top of the enemies list.

Which means I can meet with Kelly Mason again. Keep her updated, maybe over lunch. Maybe over drinks.

If the councilman had made a bigger deal out of me staring at his blueprint, I'd have asked how anyone could make sense of all that blue ink. The answer is, *I* could. I worked a few summers in the building trade before I married. Besides, anyone can read an address, writ large in the upper corner. The blueprint on the councilman's desk was for a building remodel on the corner of Main and Mountain. I know the location.

Mo Brown's Downtown Chicken.

Chapter Seven
Face in a Book

"We have art in order not to die of the truth."
~Friedrich Nietzsche

I finish my day planting seeds. Later, perhaps much later, flowers will bloom. This is how I think of investigative work that doesn't yield immediate or visible returns. My positive approach seems more constructive than the suspicion I've wasted every single second of the day.

It's a paradox, I suppose. I am not a patient man. Boxing is immediate. One way or the other, the fight is decided after a few three-minute rounds. Yet, I went to school and earned a degree—four years on a treadmill. I read books, perhaps the most sedentary of all recreations. And I chose a profession that demands long, persistent hours with no guarantee of a payoff. If I were a patient man, I might consider the implications of this.

I researched the woman Walter is seeing, using her address as a starting point. Zoey Duncan, twenty-eight years old, is an executive assistant for Winderman Construction, one of the largest contractors in the area. Graduated from the University of Colorado in Boulder with a degree in communication. Married to Lance Duncan for six years. He's an accountant. They don't have any children. She likes to post selfies in a bathing suit. She's photogenic.

I drove to the Winderman office, located Zoey's Prius, and hunkered down to wait. She left the building just after five p.m.—punctual—and drove straight home. I parked half a block away from her house and waited for her to leave again, but her husband's car was in the driveway. After a while, I gave up, impatient.

I'd hoped she'd meet Walter. I don't need photos to present my case to Kelly, but they would help.

Having wasted half the night, I head to the Tap and Wing for a few drinks and some silent contemplation. I need to think and plan. Something about the bar's dark wood and soft music quiets the mind.

Bad news waits for me. The notice on the front door informs me the business has closed, thanking me for my patronage over the years. I look at it for a long while, as if the words might rearrange and invite me in for free drinks.

The sun is already low on the horizon. The trees at the front of the building are ready for the change of seasons—the leaves look exhausted, like they're barely hanging on. I shiver a little and head home.

Once I'm inside the apartment building, I check the mailbox. I plan to do this at least once a week, but I don't always succeed. Experience tells me there's nothing good waiting for me, and I am willing to postpone the bad. But today, the little box is jammed full.

The stack of headaches dumped on my desk, unopened, I sit with my back to the window. Sasha nestles onto my foot, which is medicine I need. That, and a shot.

I log my case notes in two different spiral notebooks, one each for Minnie and Kelly. When I finish, I take Sasha for a potty break. Then we return to the half room, climb up onto the bed, turn on the tiny reading lamp, and pick a book from the shelf.

I am an eclectic reader. Why limit yourself to one kind of book? I collect different genres for different moods, both fiction and non-fiction (though the distinction between the two blurs). As with clients and witnesses, authors all lie. The careful reader knows this and keeps it in mind while flipping pages.

Except for me, of course. I won't lie to you.

Tonight, I'm feeling melancholy. I trace my fingers across the spines of books, settling on a well-worn copy of *Flowers for Algernon*, the story of a developmentally challenged man who becomes a great intellect following an experimental medical procedure. Unfortunately, the procedure's effects are short-lived, and the man loses himself, piece by piece. In the end, he struggles—and fails—to remember how to read. Saddest book ever written.

Goodbye Tap and Wing. With our favorite spot gone, Billotte and I will have to find somewhere else to drink. Somewhere Billotte hasn't been kicked out of. That may prove to be a challenge.

I read to Sasha for a while. She rests her head in my lap, sprawled out over the bed as if I'd poured her there. She shows her belly, head thrown back, and I oblige her request. Her tail wags, then she falls asleep.

Humans should have tails. Then we'd know who's truly happy to see us.

Outside, another night of outrage and revelry, playing like a soundtrack to my book.

Something nags at me, and after sorting the possibilities, I recall the stack of mail on my desk. Unopened. Sasha is sleeping, and I don't want to disturb her, but my glass is empty, so I have two reasons to get up.

Doing my best not to wake her, I wander into the big room and stare at the pile of mail. Sorting is easy. Any envelope marked "Important" or "Time Sensitive" is an ad. Any "survey" is a request for a donation. Plain window envelopes addressed to me are a bill.

Unless they are a notice from my landlord.

I scan the dense font of the landlord's letter, zeroing in on the bad news. I set the letter on the desktop, pick it up, then set it down again. Eviction.

My building has been sold. The offices will be remodeled into upscale condos and sold to people who can afford the prestige of an Old Town address.

This old building strikes me as a poor candidate for gentrification. Everyone upstairs shares a single bathroom. New plumbing will be a nightmare. How can that be cost effective? Then I try to guess the price tag on refinished condos. There are eight "offices" on the second floor. Two or three condos at a million plus apiece? Plenty of money for pipes.

Finding a new apartment will be a problem. They must allow dogs, or I can't live there. I won't find anything near the center of town, not even at double the rent. How will I afford the move? I might have to get a day job.

Bartend full time. That, or get my license and become a real private investigator. That will involve classes and certification, which costs money. And time.

I reread the letter. I'm getting plenty of advance notice. A fleeting sense of relief arrives and departs, timed to the blinking of my eyes. I return to bed. Sasha is waiting, her eyes closed and tail swishing. I curl up next to her. Outside, people are singing.

My apartment is a sanctuary. Sasha and I have been hiding here for two years. We were safe. Not happy, maybe, but content. Now? We're out. The last time my situation changed in such a dramatic fashion, I came home to find my wife cheating. That ugly moment sent me into a tailspin. The letter on the desk in the other room has given me flashbacks.

Outside, the sound of shattering glass makes me lurch in bed. Why would anyone buy a luxury apartment with that kind of nonsense going on outside? And then, like a thunderclap, comes a realization. The city could stop the protests at any time. Sweep the plaza with security. Let the police department come in and actually make arrests. Let the demonstrations at the homeless shelter go untouched, if they like, thereby shifting the protests north into the Latino community. Make new speeches with the same somber tones once used to defend protests: *Lawlessness cannot be tolerated. It's a matter of public safety.* So much the better that both stances—the importance of protest and the doctrine of non-violence—are regarded as moral high ground.

Then, sell the condos. Make money.

Put me on the street.

Am I crazy? Am I going to spend the night huddled with my dog, imagining dark forces aligned against me?

To hell with that. I pitch myself from the bed and head back to my desk. I deal with this crisis like any good, red-blooded American would. I pour myself another glass of whiskey and raise the blinds.

The show unfolds in the plaza below. The same trash can has burned for three nights running. Someone thinks it's a fire pit. I raise my glass, toasting the crowd. I resent the noise, of course. But part of me hopes they'll go on a rampage, convincing the new owners of my building of the horrible mistake they've made by evicting me. Otherwise, the crowd is welcome to burn it all to the ground. Either way, I'm on my way out.

More broken glass. More singing. If you listen closely, the shattered glass and voices provide an unlikely harmony. The next time someone dies, and I end up in church, I'll bring champagne flutes to smash in the pews. Fuck.

*   *   *   *   *

Having spent the night awake, I take Sasha for a morning walk. The sun looks like a blood orange suspended in wildfire smoke. Pretty. Sasha does her business like a good girl, then I go back to bed.

I will meet Kelly Mason for lunch in two days and would like to have something to tell her. I catch two hours of shuteye, down three Ibuprofen, a pint of Gatorade, and eat half a leftover bagel. I promise Sasha I'll be home soon (she is used to my lies) and head down the stairs.

The first name on Kelly's list of enemies is Mo Brown, owner of Downtown Chicken, on the corner of Main and Mountain. Picture a big Black man with a huge bald head sinking so far into his shoulders that to hit him with an uppercut would involve going in through his sternum. His biceps are as big around as my thighs. He has a tattoo on the left side of his neck. Looks terrible, like he had a roommate do the ink.

I know some things about Mo from my contacts in the bar business. He grew up on the East Coast, thugging. One day, he got a tryout with an arena football team. The team was impressed, took his cell number, and told him they'd get back to him in a day or two. Excited, he went to his favorite bar to celebrate, got in a fight, and fell down a stairway, tearing his ACL. Two months later, he was doing time in county for assault, wearing a knee brace.

He eventually came west with a nest egg, source unknown, and opened his restaurant. Downtown chicken is comfort food central. Fried chicken, rotisserie chicken, barbecued or otherwise. Lots of trendy side dishes, like chickpea salads, sweet potato fries, and roasted brussels sprouts. Local beers and spirits. Desserts too large for any one person to eat. Great location with lots of floor space and a modern kitchen, which so far has kept the health department from winning the war against him. I used to think the Chamber of Commerce liked having a Black owner in the middle of their white-bread town.

Now, something's changed. The newspaper says the conflict concerns air flow—exhaust fans or cold air return, or both. The county closed the doors to the restaurant more than once, demanding upgrades. Brown went public, accusing the Department of Health and Environment of racial targeting.

Downtown Chicken is a five-minute walk from my place, and the food is good. My buddy Lloyd works evenings there, so I catch the restaurant in late afternoon, after the shift change. I walk by the wait station. From there, I can see the cook's window. Lloyd's head bobs around the opening like he's fighting flyweight. I tire of waiting for him to notice me. "Lloyd!"

He freezes and looks up. When he recognizes me, he smiles and waves. "Hey, Slag."

"I'm having dinner. Come out and say hello when you get a chance."

He shakes his head. "Dinnertime, man."

"Okay, then. Get back to work."

The hostess seats me at a corner table with my back to the windows. I study the menu, but I know what I'm going to have. What I always have. Fried chicken tenders and sweet potato fries with ranch dressing.

Mo stalks the floor, grinning at customers. I look at his smile and wonder about the man's bite radius. When he gets to my table, he asks if I'm enjoying my chicken.

"My favorite thing. Best in town."

His grin widens. "That's what we like to hear."

I point at the food like it's miraculous. Like the chicken on my plate is rising from the dead instead of being eaten. "It's *fabulous.* I don't suppose you'd give me the recipe?"

His laugh is a cannon shot.

"I didn't think so. I'll have to keep coming in, I guess." I pause. "My buddy works for you. Lloyd? He says everything in your kitchen is scratch. You don't cut corners."

"No corners cut. Ever."

"I hate to think this place might be gone soon."

The sentence comes out wrong.

Mo's expression undergoes a transformation. His lip curls up just a bit. His eyes darken, as if someone gave the dimmer switch a half turn. "You know something I don't?" His tone is an octave lower.

Mistake. What I'd just said could be taken as a threat. Apparently, my encounter with Santiago taught me nothing. I push on without thinking (an important character trait if you wonder at my behavior). "I heard you're having trouble with Health and Environment. Might have to sell out. I know the community center is interested."

The flinch is visible. He looks left, right, then leans forward. "Go on."

I shrug. "I just hope they don't shut you down."

His whisper is terse. "Who the fuck are you?"

I point at my plate again. "I'm a fan of your food."

"Why would you mention the community center?"

Why? To see your reaction. Can't take it back now. "I have a friend who works down there. They're all talking about moving. You ever been there? The place smells like socks. I heard they might move here."

"How could they move here if I'm already here?"

I take a bite of chicken and chew. To my surprise, Mo folds his arms and waits.

I sigh. "Now that I think of it, they couldn't move, could they? Must be a stupid rumor."

"That so?"

I don't answer. I still have some chicken in my mouth.

"I said, is that so?" He leans in even closer. "Did the Councilman send you here?"

By now, his nose is about six inches from mine, which pisses me off. "Why are you in my face? You need to back the fuck up."

I can't believe my mouth said that.

Mo pulls back—a little—and smiles. His lids slide down halfway over his eyes, and his lips pull back taut, like a lizard. A 275-pound lizard with fists the size of hams.

There are times when I speak out of turn. If you live alone, with a dog, you lose your filter. Your mouth moves, independent of your brain. A smart man would keep his mouth shut, knowing he has things to lose. I don't have much to lose, and I'm not that smart. I wish I hadn't dropped Lloyd's name, though. I hope Mo doesn't fire him.

Mo stands still, reptile smile in place. I imagine anger pumping through his veins like acid. His temple throbs. His neck swells. He folds his arms over his chest.

I've been in the ring with men who wanted to knock me out. Hurt me. I once had a bar fight with a man who tried to cut me with a broken bottle. I don't get scared easily. But Mo Brown is big enough to hurt me by accident, and right now, he's being very intentional. "You need to get out of here. Now."

I cast a mournful glare at my half-eaten food. "You aren't going to let me finish?"

He shakes his head no. "Food's on the house. Now get the fuck out of here and don't come back."

I go. No reason not to. I have what I came for. His reaction to me spoke volumes. As I pass him by, I shudder involuntarily. I don't like to be punched from behind. I can almost feel the blow, but that's just my imagination.

* * * * *

I spend the rest of the evening tailing Zoey Duncan. She does not go home immediately, so I have high hopes she'll visit Walter. Instead, she shops for clothing. She's surprisingly frugal, avoiding boutique shops in favor of Target. After forty minutes of staring at the storefront—long enough to make me wonder if she's meeting Walter nearby—she returns carrying two bags of clothing. Next, she stops at the grocery store, coming out with a single bag of groceries.

Then home.

Frustrated, I return to Sasha. After her walk, I settle down with another book—this time, Cormac McCarthy's *The Road*. I read a passage to Sasha. The world has ended, and a father and son are wandering the apocalypse. At one point, they discover a farmhouse with people chained in the basement, some partially dismembered, being held as food for their captors. Sasha seems unimpressed with the prose, so I put the book away and tear open a pack of treats, which she devours with great enthusiasm.

Chapter Eight
A Thousand Ships are Launched

"A particularly beautiful woman is a source of terror. As a rule, a beautiful woman is a terrible disappointment."
~Carl Jung

Kelly Mason asks to meet me for lunch, rather than returning to my office. I wonder at her motivation. Is my office too shabby? Does my Cave of the Winds clock invoke memories of a bad visit to Colorado Springs? Perhaps she wants to get to know me. A nice, comfortable lunch. Good conversation.

Probably the cave.

She chooses a Mexican food place up the road from Downtown Chicken, a place I jokingly think of as *Casa del Casa*. Not real Mexican food. Tomatoes and lettuce instead of lime and cilantro in the tacos. No corn husks on the tamales. Students like the frozen margaritas, served in glasses the size of a fishbowl, so the place stays open.

I arrive five minutes early, but Kelly is already seated, waiting for me. Her hands are folded on the tabletop. I slow my pace. No use seeming anxious. "Hello," I say, funneling my charm into a cheery voice, rather than a clever choice of greeting.

She nods.

I sit down and turn directly to the menu. "What's good here?"

"I don't know your tastes, Mr. Ferguson."

"Call me Slag."

Her gaze narrows. "I don't think so."

I try not to frown.

"Slag is a nickname for a boy, don't you think? I'm hoping I hired a professional." She tilts her head, staring at my face. "I'm sorry if I seem rude, but you've been on the job for a week, and I'm anxious to find out what you've learned."

I nod. "Fair enough. Let's get down to business."

That's when my friend Jillian comes by to take our order. Proud Latina with beautiful hair and a killer smile. We worked together for a couple months at Wesley's. She moved on when she couldn't get enough hours. "Hey, Slag. What's up? You drinking today?"

I pass on alcohol, not wishing to confirm Kelly's suspicions about my professionalism. Ordering food at the *Casa* is a crap shoot. "Give me something with *camarones*, please."

Jillian brushes a loose strand of black hair from her eyes. "Believe it or not, we don't have shrimp. Not even tacos."

I snort. "Okay. Give me something covered in cheese."

"That's everything on the menu," she laughs. "Try the smothered burrito. It's not bad."

Kelly orders a salad and iced tea. She's watching her figure.

So am I.

With Jillian gone, I start my pitch. "I have a good idea why they are threatening Walter. And I think I know what they're threatening him with. As for who's behind it—I have a good idea about that, too."

"Go on."

"I believe your husband is involved in a touchy real estate transaction involving the community center. The city's plans have put your husband in conflict with other parties. They are likely blackmailing him."

"Blackmail?"

I shrug. "I haven't confirmed all the details. I'd prefer to present the specifics of the case to you when I've finished. And I expect to finish soon."

"I'd prefer the specifics now."

The woman knows what she wants. Or thinks she does. "Okay. Mo Brown looks like your culprit. You listed him as a potential enemy. He's got a criminal background, and he's battling Health and Environment over his restaurant. I have a witness that heard him threaten to kill someone. That might be bluster, or it might be real. I had a confrontation with Mr. Brown myself, but the discussion was not conclusive."

Kelly sat back, silent. "A witness?"

"One of his employees."

"And you talked to Mr. Brown?"

"Sort of. He threw me out of his restaurant the second I pressed him on the problems with your husband's department."

Silence. I wait, staring. The harsh light through the big front window is kinder to her than to the rest of the diners. Cool skin, like poured cream. Eyes the color of blueberries. I'm reminded of a movie, but I keep it to myself. For now.

"So, you have made some progress. Thank you."

I try not to show how pleased I am.

"How do we stop him?"

With a picture of Mo in my mind, I wonder how to stop a runaway train. Waving my hand, I say, "First things first. I need to be sure Mo is behind what's happening."

That's when Jillian returns with our plates. The burrito looks good. I'd normally wolf the thing down and move on, but I'm not anxious to end lunch early. Eat slow, I tell myself, which reminds me of Walter and his tiny, mincing bites.

"They're very fast here," Kelly comments after Jillian leaves.

"They probably microwave everything."

"Is that a bad thing?" The question seems sincere.

"Not if you're in a hurry." I take my first bite of the burrito. Jillian was right. It's edible.

"Is your food okay?" she asks. This is her first personal question, and I take that as a positive sign. I nod. She takes a bite of her salad, chews a requisite number of times and swallows, takes a sip of water, then sits back. "You said you knew what they were blackmailing Walter with. What did you mean?"

This woman is razor sharp.

"I'd rather not say, in case I'm wrong. I'll know soon enough, though."

"Are you saying my husband is dirty? Involved in illegal activity? Because I won't believe that. I know better."

Your husband is a government employee. Of course, he's dirty. I take a bite and chew, giving myself time to craft an answer. "Look, I know you want answers, but I'm not going to lay out the case until I'm sure of every aspect. I want to be sure before I flap my lips. I told you about Mo because I didn't want you to think I was sitting on my hands, racking up hours."

She shook her head. "I wouldn't think that."

"You might."

A hint of a smile. "Mr. Billotte insisted you were an honorable man." She pauses. "When I first visited your office, I was a bit put off. But after thinking about it, I decided that anyone with an office like yours was either completely incompetent or very honest." She paused again. "You seem to know what you're doing, so..."

"Thanks." My face flushes hot. Honorable? No, not completely. I'm glad she can't read my mind.

She turns to her salad and digs in. I'm surprised. She has an appetite. That seems like an invitation to reintroduce myself to Mr. Burrito, which I do with gusto.

After another sip of water, she asks, "Do you like your job?"

"Yeah, I do. I like meeting new people."

"So, being a private investigator is like being a church greeter?"

I burst out laughing, and she smiles, too, and it's as if someone cranked up the sun.

"Here's a random question," I say. "Have you ever watched the movie, *High Noon*?"

Her smile falters. "I don't think so."

"It's a famous western."

"I don't recall. Why do you ask?"

"You look a little like the actress who played the sheriff's wife."

"I'm sorry. I don't know the movie." I study her face and wonder if she's lying. That would be a clever way to avoid acknowledging a compliment.

She's back to her salad, nearly finished. She doesn't seem like someone who orders dessert, so our meeting may end soon.

"You asked if I liked my job. I do. People in trouble come to me with problems they can't solve themselves." I think of Minnie. "And I help them. I *fix* things."

She seems to be studying me. At last, she says, "That's a very male answer."

"How so?"

She shakes her head and puts down her fork. "Men like to solve problems, don't they?"

"We do, I suppose. I do, anyway."

And just like that, Jillian is at the table, selling dessert. Kelly declines and asks for the tab. Jillian drops separate checks. Kelly clearly made arrangements before I arrived. We're uncomfortably silent as we wait for our credit cards to be processed. When Jillian returns with thanks and the cards, Kelly takes hers, makes a quick mental calculation, fills out the receipt, and slips her card back into her clutch purse.

"I'll keep you posted," I promise.

"I still have my one question," she says. "When you know for sure who is threatening my husband, what will you do to protect him?"

"Depends on the threat. Different situations call for different solutions."

"What if someone intends to hurt Walter physically?"

"I won't let that happen."

The worry at the corner of her eyes seems to soften. "Thank you," she whispers. Her voice gives me chills. If she told me I should set myself on fire with that same whisper, I might reach for a lighter.

I sit still for a minute, waiting until Kelly leaves the building and crosses the big window on the way to her car. Then I flip open the faux-leather check holder to see how much she tipped. You can tell a lot about someone by how they tip. Besides, Jillian is a friend. If Kelly Mason stiffed her, I'll make up the difference.

Twenty-five percent. Go figure.

* * * * *

Friday with Billotte happens at a brew pub in one of Old Town's alleys. The place is small, with just three tables inside—all taken. We plant outside at the porch rail and drink pale ale. The house appetizers are meant to be upscale, so there's a lot of flatbread and hummus and not much flavor. The evening is crisp, not cold. I can smell fall coming. Cinnamon and dead leaves.

Billotte burps and wipes his mouth with his sleeve. "So, you're all fired up about Kelly Mason."

There's a conversation starter. I sniff the wind. "She's a beautiful woman. And smart. Too smart."

"Kind of flat-chested."

"Athletic," I say, correcting him.

"She's got to be evil, right?"

I frown. "How evil is she? You go to church with her."

Billotte affects a solemn tone. "You ever know a Catholic girl who behaved?"

"Come on. You know her. What do you think of her?"

I've asked a serious question, and Billotte answers seriously. "I think any woman who looks like that is used to getting everything she wants. Must change a person." He pauses to finish his beer. "If I could get anything I wanted, I'd be a different guy."

"You'd get laid more."

"And fired less," he adds. "So, when are you going to hire me?"

"Can't do it."

"Why not?" He scratches his ear. "Answer me this. How many clients do you have now?"

I know where this is going.

"How many?" he repeats.

"Two."

"Two. And how many would you have if I hadn't steered them to you?"

"I thank you for that. I really do. . . *Bobo*."

Billotte grumbles, "Minnie has a big mouth."

"Yes, Minnie." She'd tipped me off to a nickname for Billotte that wasn't *asshole* or *jerkoff*.

"Were you able to do anything for her? With Santiago?"

"I talked to him and told him to stay away."

Billotte shakes his head. "Today?"

"Two days ago."

"Oh. Because he showed up drunk at her door last night. Scared her pretty bad."

I can feel bile at the back of my throat. "Son of a bitch."

"When you talked to him, what did you say?"

"I asked him to back off. As a favor."

Billotte winces. I can tell he thinks I screwed up. "You can't be polite with those guys. They'll think you're being weak."

"I wanted to show some respect," I say. "His friends were watching."

Billotte adds a groan to his wince. "You can't talk to him in front of his crew. He'll put up a front if they're watching."

"But he's never alone," I say.

"I *know*. That's why I sent her to you. It's a touchy situation."

After ordering another round, Billotte asks, "You ever hear of vendetta?"

"Italian style vendetta? I've read about it."

"Italians can carry on a blood feud for generations. It never ends. You're *obligated* to keep killing." He sips his beer and shoves flatbread into his mouth. "This shit isn't bad. Hummus is made of beans. Did you know that? Anyway, Mexicans are the same way."

"*All* Mexicans, right?" I love goading Billotte.

He ignores me and continues. "You can't look weak, or they'll jump you. You can't say shit in front of their crew, or they'll jump you. You can't confront them, or —"

"Okay, I get it. What *can* you do?"

"I don't know. I was hoping you'd know."

I chew on that for a minute while Billotte chews on flatbread. "So, exactly why don't you want to hire me?" he asks.

A serious question deserves a serious answer. "You ever hear someone talk about lines you don't cross?"

"Sure. Picket lines."

"That's not—"

"I'm joking. I know what you mean."

I bite my lip. Billotte is my best friend, and I'm about to insult him. "You don't have any sense about what is and what isn't appropriate. You've been fired a dozen times for fighting or just shooting your mouth off. The things I do require. . . finesse."

"Finesse?" Billotte asks. "You mean, like not talking to Santiago in front of his crew?"

Fair enough, but I'm not done answering the question. "You fight too much. You'd get both of us in a lot of trouble." He's staring at me like he doesn't understand. "You *do* fight a lot, right?"

He shakes his head. "The world is what it is. I can't change it. But if someone sticks his nose up in my mind-your-own, I'm gonna do something about it. That's all."

I nod, and down half my beer.

"I understand what you're saying," he says, looking sad.

"There's more," I tell him. "I'm not rolling in cash. You know the story of the loaves and fishes?"

"Of course. I'm a good Catholic boy."

"Well, I got a dinner roll and a minnow here. How am I supposed to feed two of us with that?"

"Well," Billotte says, and much to my relief, he drops the subject. I shift in my spot against the rail. The sun has set, and it's getting colder. A young girl comes bouncing past in sandals and shorts. I wonder why she isn't freezing.

Billotte stares after her, more out of habit than interest, I suspect. He finishes his beer and sets the glass on the porch rail. "Okay. But about the girl? Kelly?"

"Yes?"

"Just be careful she doesn't chop off your minnow because you want to give her a roll."

Chapter Nine
A Shot to the Head

"You're not born woke. Something wakes you up."
~DeRay Mckesson

Another Saturday. Another bartending shift. This one has me on edge because so many people are out and about. The sidewalks are jammed with kids dancing and jumping around. Something in the news today has made them happy, but that doesn't mean there won't be trouble. Even happy customers are a couple drinks away from stupid.

Wesley's fills up early. When Lloyd walks in, there's only one seat open at the bar—the end stool next to the wait station. Lloyd grabs the seat with a smile. Girls will be at his elbow the whole shift.

I pour a shot and set it in front of him. "This one's on me." I pause. "You still working for Big Mo?"

"Like a slave," he says, downing the shot.

"That was quick. What are you drinking next?"

"Need any more product tested?" He looks hopeful.

"Not tonight," I say. "But shots of Jack are on special."

"Sounds good to me."

I'm relieved Lloyd still has his job. Mo Brown might be spiteful enough to fire him just for knowing me.

The drinkers at the bar are burning through shots. Some try to fool me with obscure drink names, but I know all the latest concoctions. The guy sitting at Lloyd's left orders an old-school shot, and I smile. I know it. Half a shot of vodka, half a shot of white rum. Then, spoon in Irish Crème, which hangs in the liquid like a clot.

"There you go," I say. "Cum in a Hot Tub."

The drinker's friend, one more seat to the left, seems disgusted. "Damn! That's gross!"

The drinker strokes his goatee and prepares himself. I half expect him to hold his nose while he downs it.

"What the hell is that?" A woman farther down the row tries to shout over the noise at the front door. A group of eight wants dinner, and they're laughing.

"Cum in a Hot Tub," the man with the goatee shouts.

"No, it's not," the woman says, a sly smile on her face. She flips her red hair back, adding, "I've seen cum in a hot tub, and it doesn't look like that."

"We should check it out later. Davy has a hot tub."

She laughs. "Fill it with rum and vodka, and I'll see what I can do."

I'm impressed. The woman clearly knows her drinks.

The bar and restaurant are filled past capacity, and I'm getting worried. If the fire marshal comes by, he'll write me a ticket. As if I'm the guy letting everyone in. We're supposed to space the bar chairs, but Warren keeps jamming in extras. I can see the little bastard peering out from the kitchen doors now, grinning like an idiot. A packed house makes for a happy boss.

Last winter, the fire marshal came in for a head count after I'd asked the hostess to stop seating, but she said Warren told her to ignore me. In walked the fire marshal, clicker in hand. We'd already sat double our limit, filling nearly every table. I'd told Warren, "Take out some of these tables. We can't seat them all. Open up some space." He didn't listen to that advice either. While the marshal wrote me a ticket, Warren poked his head out of the kitchen, like a woodchuck leaving its burrow, hollering at me for over-seating.

Later, I handed Warren the ticket and told him to pay for it. No argument. But if I get ticketed tonight, I'll probably have to pay myself.

Things have changed. Jobs are getting scarce, and I need money to change apartments.

At the start of my shift, I asked Warren if I could pick up a couple extra shifts a week. I told him how I'm getting evicted. He was sad for me. Sadder still because there were no extra shifts for me.

Now, the guy with the goatee turns to Lloyd and says, "You must be pretty happy tonight."

Lloyd finishes a shot. "Happy enough. Saturday night."

"Yeah, that too."

I move down the row, serving more drinks. One couple wants to transfer their tab to a dinner table. Three drinks each. The tab and the tip will go to Cathy, the skinny gal with bad skin. She'll pocket the cash and wave goodbye at the end of the shift without a second thought.

I wash glasses, ramming them up and down on the bar washer brushes. The motor is dying and makes too much noise. Glancing up, I see Goatee Guy motioning for another shot.

"Same thing?"

Having gotten my attention, he takes his time. "Surprise me," he says, finally. "Give me something with Kahlua."

A shot of Kahlua? I keep the joke to myself.

Something about this guy is wrong. He's too loud. He punctuates his words with his hands, whipping them around the glassware on the bar top. He leans close to Lloyd, tapping him on the shoulder, like Lloyd was his sidekick. Lloyd is smiling, but it's that sideways smile he gives to managers at work.

Goatee likes Bailey's, so I pour him a B-52, making sure the layers show. He stares at it, shrugs, downs the shot and taps the bar. "Another. This time, give me something with liquor in it."

"You celebrating?" I ask. The guy is drinking too much, too fast. I need to slow him down.

"Bet your ass!" he says. "You heard the news, right?"

I shake my head. "I don't listen to the news."

The guy stops still. His mouth is open, and he glances to the side to see if Lloyd is watching. He's performing surprise. "You're kidding, right?"

"No, I'm not."

I don't have a television. There's a radio in the car, but I play old cassette tapes from the pawn shop. I don't explain any of this. Why bother?

"Today was an important day. The Supremes made a ruling."

"Diana Ross, or Mary Wilson?" I ask.

Lloyd swallows a laugh, and adds, "I *loved* Diana Ross. Her voice was like silk. Just smooth, and..." He wipes his lips with the back of his shirt sleeve. "Like silk."

I pour Lloyd another shot, so I can ignore the guy at his elbow. "Not me. I liked Jean Terrell and Mary Wilson," I say. "The album they did after Diana Ross went solo is the best Supremes album ever. "Up the Ladder to the Roof" is their best song."

"Better than "Someday We'll be Together"? You're crazy, Slag." Lloyd is suddenly serious, looking old and melancholy, like a trumpet player at a New Orlean's funeral. Makes me feel like I disappointed a favorite drunken uncle.

The man at his elbow slaps both palms on the bar top. "What's wrong with you two?"

I have a glass and a towel in my hand. I set both down.

"The Supreme Court makes a fucking landmark decision, and you guys are talking songs from the sixties?"

I give him credit. He got the decade right.

The guy swivels in his seat, facing Lloyd. "Come on, man, that court decision was for *you*. You get that, don't you? It was for *your people*." He turns back to me, staring. His voice lowers a bit, which I think is supposed to be menacing. "I know it don't mean shit to *you*."

True enough. I know the decision has something to do with race. I don't care to know more.

What I do care about is a customer who's had too much to drink. That's okay. We're in a restaurant with a bar. Half the people here are crossing the line. The world can go to hell in a basket, and people will still drink. A few laughs, a chance to hook up, and most of the time, nothing worse than a headache the next day.

He leans over the bar counter, closer to me. I expect him to demand another drink, but he surprises me. "Your time is done, and you don't even know it. That's because you're a drone. Not the kind that flies around. The kind that moves through life with nothing on your mind but yourself. You don't know what's going on around you, and you don't give a shit. Well, the future's coming for you, and there's nothing you can do about it."

Lloyd is hammered enough to try and defend me. He nudges the man. "Hey, come on. Slag's a good guy. We used to work together."

"Yeah? What did you do?"

"I was a dishwasher."

"And what did he do?"

Lloyd points at me like I was a slide presentation. "Slag is a bartender."

"There you go," says Goatee. "I know the pecking order in restaurants. It's good you get along with the boss man."

I glance at Lloyd. He sits back. His eyebrows are as far up his forehead as they'll go, and his mouth is open.

I tap the bar top in front of the man with the Goatee. "You've had a lot to drink. I think you're through for the evening."

When you cut a drinker off, they almost always react in anger. One way to handle the situation is to appeal to friends. I turn to the guy's buddy. "It's time to get your friend home safe."

"Fuck that," the friend says.

The man with the goatee smiles.

I shrug. "I won't be serving either of you any more alcohol."

"I want to see your manager," they say, almost in unison.

"If he comes by, I'll flag him down." I don't wait for an answer. I grab the man's credit card from the stack next to the computer, close out the tab and flip Goatee his card. I won't need a signature. There'll be no tip. I'll write *signature on file* when I run the slip. If he wants to fight the charge, he'll find out how important customer service is to credit card companies.

Meanwhile, one of the waitresses drops a drink ticket for the party of eight. I move to the right and start filling her order. Lots of umbrella drinks, so I'm locked down for a minute. Next, I move to the far end of the bar and pour drinks for the people there. With my back to the bar, I stand at the computer screen, adding drinks to the respective tabs. That's when I hear breaking glass.

Either the man with the goatee or his buddy knocked a glass off the bar top, shattering it in my dish sink. I'm going to have to drain the suds, pick the glass out of the basin, and refill.

The woman with the red hair stands up, shaking her head. "I'm out of here."

The buddy says, "Sorry about that." He's not sorry.

Lloyd looks at me. "These guys are out of control."

The man with the goatee turns to Lloyd, leaning into his face. "You're siding with him?"

Lloyd shrugs.

"Time to go," I tell Goatee and his buddy.

"I don't think so."

I take off my apron. "I'm going to come around the end of the bar. If I get to you, I'm going to hurt you." I toss the apron over the cash register and start walking.

"You better go," Lloyd says.

"I'll go when I'm ready."

Lloyd shakes his head. "Get ready."

The buddy grabs his friend and starts pulling. "Come on, man. Fuck this. It's not worth it."

The man with the goatee allows himself to be pulled away. He points at Lloyd. "You need to think about what just happened here." Then, he points at me. "And you need to wake the fuck up."

Lloyd is silent.

The closer I get, the quicker the two men move. Goatee pauses at the door to flip me off, and then he's gone, shuffling into the crowd like a card into a deck.

It takes me a moment to return and don my apron. I need the time to settle my adrenaline. Lloyd sits, staring at the empty shot glass in front of him.

I clear my throat. "They have an appetizer special tonight. Chicken wings fried in duck fat. Got a fancy name for it, but that's really all they are. Worth trying if you've never had them before. Get you a plate?"

"Nah. I gotta go." He stands up.

"Shot for the road?"

Lloyd sits back down. "Always room for one more, I guess."

I pour him another Jack. I hate the look on his face. Drawn in, like part of his insides just went hollow. Lloyd is a working man, trying to enjoy a few drinks after a shift in a hot kitchen. All he wants is to be left alone. "Thanks for sticking up for me," I say. "I got your tab."

"I didn't do anything," he mumbles.

"Yeah, you did." I grab a bar towel and start wiping the spot where Goatee had been drinking. "Let me ask you something. When we worked together, did I act like I was your boss?"

Lloyd scratches his chin stubble. "Truth?"

"Always."

"You acted like you were the *manager's* boss. You're a know-it-all son of a bitch."

I laugh. "But you like me, right?"

Lloyd taps the bar top. "Keep pouring, boss."

* * * * *

The bad taste in my mouth lasts well beyond the end of the shift. The fire marshal never shows, but the rest of the evening is a nightmare. Weak tips. Rude customers. And the jerk with the goatee? Ugly business.

Old Town Plaza is empty tonight, so I take Sasha for a long walk. With nobody to bother us, she's free to sniff the doorways of closed businesses and leave her mark on every plant jutting up through the asphalt. Night walks seem to energize her, and she has a bounce in her step that cheers me up. Since she's enjoying herself, I keep going, which gives me time to think.

I know what's *really* bothering me.

A light rain starts to fall. Sasha rams her nose at the base of a trash can, and I can't pull her away, so I stop and let her explore. Off to the left, a newspaper lays, rolled and bound by a rubber band, in what's quickly becoming a rain puddle near the front step of the jewelry store. Hardly enough news to stand up to the rubber band. When Sasha moves on, I bend and scoop the little thing, shake it off, and jam it into my coat pocket. Maybe I'll dry it off at home and read up on the Supremes. Or maybe I'll throw it away.

A little background is in order. When my ex-wife and I parted ways, we split the savings account. She ended up sticking me with the legal fees for the divorce, but they weren't all that much, and I didn't have the heart to fight. If we'd had kids like we planned, things might have been different. As it was, the cut was quick and clean, like a battlefield amputation.

I left my day job shortly after the breakup. I couldn't seem to haul my ass out of bed for a few months, and besides, I had enough money to drink and pay rent. But I kept my part-time gig at the bar. I wasn't sleeping nights anyway.

Businesses were hiring private security, so I found odd jobs here and there. I'd been a bouncer, so I was vaguely qualified. I had a concealed carry permit for years—personal preference—but I didn't need a gun for the jobs I took, thanks to my fists.

The next thing I know, two years go by, and I'm still bartending and doing part-time security work. Two years gone.

"Let's get home, Sasha." The rain is coming down harder. In another few weeks, the rain might turn to snow. You never know in Colorado. I pull Sasha's leash in the direction of Old Town Plaza, and she doesn't seem to mind. Her fur is soaked. She'll be shaking rain all over the apartment floor. My fogged brain tries to come up with a joke about Sasha making it rain—a stripper's joke—but there's no joy in it.

Back at the apartment, I give Sasha a treat and settle down at my desk. I pull out the local paper and lay it flat. Too wet to read. I open up the browser in my cellphone and start visiting news sites. After a while, I feel the need for a drink. I fetch a glass and half a bottle of Pennington's, but I keep reading.

Mr. Goatee was right. I'm disconnected. I've been a drone.

It's going to be a long night.

Chapter Ten
Travels in the Sheep-Eat-Sheep World

"Tenured professors are more prone than the rest of us to think that the university is the universe."
~Pankaj Mishra

I visit the campus three times before I catch Professor Linderman during posted office hours. He's the next subject on Kelly Mason's enemies list, sitting at his desk, door open. I rap on the door frame to get his attention. He looks up at me through round, wire-rim glasses and gives me a small, cupid smile with pursed lips. "Yes?"

I introduce myself as Mark Ferguson, freelance writer. I explain that I'm researching an article on the Department of Health and Environment.

"I am a Cultural Studies professor," he says. "I think you might want to talk to someone in Natural Sciences."

"Oh, I will. But I got your name because you clashed with Health and Environment about the purchase of some research equipment, and I wanted to hear about it from you."

The professor glances at his watch. He's deciding whether to talk to me. Could go either way. He has forty-five minutes left in his posted hour, but I'm not a student. He runs his long, tapered fingers through his wispy hair, rubs at a watery eye, then sighs.

I'm in.

I take a chair. The office is tiny—the size of a small bedroom, or a large closet. Framed diplomas and various awards cover one wall. The other wall is taken up by a bookcase, stuffed so full that books are stacked sideways atop other books. A window looks out over the University Library and a flower planter. The perennials are dying. My ex-wife, the florist, would weep.

"Thanks for your time," I say. "I'm counting on someone to give me a straight story." An appeal for honesty might help me. I flip open a spiral notebook and pull out a pen. "So, as I understand it, Health and Environment required a certain kind of equipment, and you objected to being required to purchase equipment from a company owned by the head of H and E. Is that right?"

"No, that's not right." He pauses, as if wondering whether to bother. Then, with a groan, he launches into an extended soliloquy. "The purchase of equipment is complex. The government defines equipment as tangible, nonexpendable property with a useful life of more than one year and an acquisition cost of $5,000 or more per unit. That covers a great number of purchases. The federal guidelines governing equipment run more than 1,300 pages. State guidelines, which extend additional protections, are more than 1,100 pages. It's not always clear whether a piece of equipment is in compliance. Manufacturers don't always care. For example, a piece of equipment manufactured in Michigan may not be compliant with Colorado regulations. The onus should be on the manufacturer to produce a compliant product, but the pursuit of profits and ethical concerns seldom coincide."

Linderman pauses and gives me another pursed smile. He's slumped in his chair like a jellyfish. Either he's extremely relaxed or his spine is failing. "Because research facilities cannot depend on ethical manufacturers, they must vet their purchases. Researchers are not compliance experts, as a rule, so a subset industry has developed within the compliance field to help navigate the difficult waters of equipment purchases."

My pen, poised, is inactive thus far.

"I had an objection to Health and Environment's dictates in this regard. I hasten to express my admiration in general for the job done by the department. Public safety is a crucial governmental service. However, they insisted on running University purchases past a certain compliance company that happened to be owned, at least in part, by the head of Health and Environment."

"Walter Mason?"

Linderman's face sours for a moment. "Yes, Mr. Mason." He pulls back, his head sinking into his shoulders. His chin disappears.

"So, he wanted the University to use his consulting firm?"

"An ethical conundrum. The sort of consideration that the business world tramples on a daily basis. Government, however, ought to hold itself to a higher standard. I voiced my objection, and that should have been the end of it."

"But it wasn't."

"No, alas. I was asked my opinion and gave it honestly. Professors in other departments, including Physics and Animal Science, both of whom purchase a great deal of equipment, were asked for their opinions as well, but journalists are drawn to questions of ethics, so of course, they quoted me. As it turned out, those quotes were the fulcrum upon which the story rested." He paused again, frowning. "Who did you say you write for?"

"I freelance," I say, and rush on to change the subject. "What was Walter Mason's response to your criticism?"

Again, the sour face, like a mouthful of vinegar. "He questioned the relevance of my opinions. As if cultural studies weren't the hub upon which the wheel of higher learning attaches itself, spoke by spoke." He dismisses the thought with a wave. "Stuart Hall said, *Identity is never singular but is multiply constructed across intersecting and antagonistic discourses, practices and positions.* Questions of existence, along with their answers, spring from cultural studies. Ethics are an important subset of those concerns. So, certainly, I would argue in favor of the appropriateness of any comment I happened to have made."

I nod and scribble a line on my pad that morphs into a zig-zag pattern. If he keeps talking much more, I'm going to jab my pen in my ear.

"At any rate, the disagreement was much ado about nothing," Linderman continued. He straightened his brown tie. "Mr. Mason and I have moved beyond the initial unpleasantness. We are both successful within our respective realms and have no need to continue the disagreement. I find I must reserve my efforts of a fiercer nature for interdepartmental politics. Should you ever happen to write an article on that subject, I would prove to be a *marvelous* source." He glances up. A young girl has stopped in his doorway. "Now, can I do anything else for you?" he asks me.

"Oh," the girl says, as if surprised someone beside herself might visit the professor. She's a cute blond with a single dimple, dressed in a short black skirt and white sweater. She projects a studied innocence, with open eyes and a trusting smile. "Am I interrupting?" Of course, she is. A decade ago, she'd have all my attention. Today, she is an unwelcome disruption.

"I think we're about through here," Professor Linderman says. His flat, watery eyes have come to life, and he sits straight in his chair. I am relieved to see his spine is intact. He turns to me. "You were done, weren't you?"

"Actually, I had another question, if you don't mind."

Lindeman looks up at the girl and says, "Don't go anywhere." Then he glares at me.

"You mentioned you've patched things up with Walter Mason. Do you happen to have his cellphone number?"

Lindeman's face registers impatience. No sign of recognition. "No." He glances at the girl. "Why would I? My acquaintance with Mr. Mason does not extend to personal calls." Lindeman is clearly irritated now, though I'm sure he doesn't want to reveal it to his audience. "I'm certain you can reach Mr. Mason at his office, after all."

So much for Lindeman calling Walter Mason at home.

I offer the professor my thanks and leave him to the young girl. I hope she gets an A.

As I walk to the stairway, I watch students rush by. Smooth skin. Reckless clothing. Racing through uncertain hallways, gazes fixed forward as if the future were just ten steps away. I envy them all. I'm more than a decade older than these bright faces. How can that be?

Luckily, my trip to the campus wasn't wasted. I'm able to cross Professor Linderman off the list of enemies. At first glance, he seems harmless. And he didn't flinch when asked about Walter Mason's phone. But the clincher?

Men who talk that much seldom act. They are too much in love with their voices to move forward, content to narrate the past as if their words and their thoughts mattered.

* * * * *

Years ago, I spent one semester and part of another at Colorado State University. The desire to get core classes out of the way did battle with the desire to learn something enjoyable. I mixed math and physics with Introduction to Literature and Art History. I was no good at math (which meant I was no good at physics), but I struggled through. The liberal arts courses were the real disappointment.

What is literature? The introductory lecture made it clear that anything qualified. Novels. Poetry. Laundry lists. Grocery receipts. All could be used as cultural documents—entry points for ideological discussions.

In art class, the professor showed slides. Michelangelo's frescos. Pollack's paint splashes. Duchamp's urinal. Since everything is art, and art is everything, the student is spared the effort of discrimination. Or thought.

Meanwhile, I tended bar. Things are different in the real world. My dry martini has two drops of dry vermouth. The traditional recipe calls for one part vermouth and two parts gin, but if you serve that in a bar today, you'll be out of a job.

Customers discriminate. Not every drink is good. Some are shit.

I didn't regret the lost tuition money when I left college. I'd learned a valuable lesson. I still wanted an education, so I got myself a library card.

* * * * *

Later, Walter Mason leaves work to go to lunch. Once he's off the lot, I pay his office a visit. Having passed the metal detectors without having to resort to a cavity search, I am once again Mark Ferguson, freelance writer. Simone, Walter's receptionist, does not seem to recognize me. Good. I ask to speak to Walter. Instead, I'm introduced to Naomi Adriana, which was, of course, my intent all along. Hers is the last name on Kelly Mason's list, and though I have my doubts about her culpability, I intend to interview her.

Perched behind her desk, she rises when I enter the room. The act of standing does not perceptively increase her height. She wears a shapeless dress full of bright shapes and colors—the patterns with which clothing designers hope to distract from the wearer's weight. She is a plain woman with short-cut hair and a stern face. She doesn't seem to be wearing any jewelry.

Her face seems familiar to me.

Having been introduced by Simone the receptionist, I sit down and face Walter Mason's right hand gal. Her office is spartan. Rigid and bare. A pair of diplomas hang behind the desk, both for achievement in the field of Human Resources. The desktop is all business. No pictures. No knickknacks. One lonely telephone and two neat piles of correspondence. A bookcase to her right boasts even rows of books and binders.

No dust anywhere.

She sits, then folds her hands atop the desk. "How may I help you, Mr. Ferguson?"

I sit, pen and pad in hand. "I'm writing an article on your department."

"Who are you writing for? And what is the angle of your article?"

I decide to answer the second question, in hopes of passing over the first. "I'm following up on the conflict between your department and Professor Linderman at the college. I understand Mr. Mason owns—"

"That is old news."

"Hence, my description of the piece as being a follow-up." I mimic the voice of Professor Linderman. Perhaps big words and a pompous tone will make me more believable as a writer.

Ms. Adriana sits back, snorting. "Well, go on then."

"I spoke to the professor just this morning. I would love to hear your side of the conflict."

"There was no conflict."

I scribble on my pad. "Professor Linderman objected to your department's use of Mr. Mason's compliance company. He felt an ethical boundary had been crossed."

"Nonsense."

"How would you describe it then?" My pen is ready.

Naomi Adriana draws a deep, ragged breath. She drums her nails on the bare desktop. At last, she says, "In the past, the safety measures for machinery were in the hands of the people who made the machines. Clearly a conflict of interest. Safety versus profit. Very bad outcome for the poor people working the machines. People were hurt, sometimes killed. Meanwhile, industrial injury became an insurance issue, rather than a safety issue. A missing limb had a specific value in the marketplace. Protections took a back seat to the commodification of loss.

"The advent of measures that actually address public safety—the reason Health and Environment exists—are relatively new. OSHA, for example, was founded in the seventies. It's not overstating the issue to say that before the Occupational Safety and Health Act of 1970, people were at the mercy of their workplaces."

"Good background information," I say. "But let me steer you back to ethical boundaries. How is public safety served by Walter Mason's self-interests?"

"Walter Mason's interests have always been in the service of the public." The words are a solemn pronouncement.

"But you do see the ethical issue, right?"

She shakes her head for emphasis. "You do see that personal and professional considerations might coincide, *right?* Has it occurred to you that Mr. Mason founded his company to provide a service that aids in the implementation of government mandates he's been charged to enforce? Is that concept so inconceivable?"

No, it's not. She has me off guard.

She pushes back her chair. "I'll be frank with you. I'm not interested in participating in gotcha journalism for someone who refuses to disclose for whom he is writing."

She noticed. Still, she's awfully combative, and I say so.

"I think we're done here."

She's right. The set of her jaw convinces me. I stand. "Well, thank you for your time."

"I know who you are."

I stop still. "Pardon?"

"You're the man with the abused dog."

Now I recognize her. Three women protesters had interrupted my walk with Sasha in the plaza. One of them—Shelly?—had been nice. This woman had not. She'd seen Sasha's ear and accused me of hurting her.

"The rescue dog," I corrected.

"So you say.

Normally, I'd let that go. But something about this woman sets me off, and I'm not inclined to let her comments pass. "You seem to know a lot about me for someone who's spoken to me once."

"I know people. And you're not very good at hiding who you are."

Since I've already lost control here, I try a Hail Mary pass. "I'll talk to your boss, instead."

Her laugh is like a drill bit through aluminum siding. "You're no journalist."

"We'll see what he says about the way his *subordinate* treats the press."

Her voice changes again. Lower, now. "I've known Walter Mason for a few years, now. He is a *very* smart man. I have absolutely no doubt he'll see you for who you are."

I leave without another word, walking down the hall past Simone the receptionist, who stares at me. I don't think she'll forget my face a second time. Too bad. Getting information from her will be problematic.

Outside, I try to calm myself. I hate passive-aggressive people. Moreso when they win the round. Naomi Adriana sparred like a pro. I walk into Old Town, breathing deep, hands on my hips.

I can feel an early fall in the air. The few trees jutting from their grated holes in the walkways have shed their leaves. A cloudy sky. Smoke from the wildfires. A sprinkling of shoppers, hands jammed in their pockets. Empty store fronts. Windows boarded up with plywood. Summer is winding down.

Something nags at me. Not just the unpleasantness. The interview with Walter's number two surprised me. Naomi Adriana is no backstabber. I'd expected her to give me some "off the record" quote about how Walter was mismanaging his department. I did not expect her proclamations of support. If she regards Walter as an enemy, she's the best actress in history.

Something else. Her office wasn't what you'd expect from someone jockeying for position. Her workspace is frugal and efficient, like it belongs to a saint, or someone on a mission. Someone married to their job. The kind of person *I'd* want to hire. Personality like a cactus? Who cares? Anyone in a number two position is a whip—a person who gets things done. I'm willing to bet she's great at her job.

And that irritates the piss out of me.

Two names off the list. Goodbye, professor. Goodbye, Naomi. A good day's work, then. Why am I still so angry? I chew on it a little more, and decide it was their shared demeanor. Both Lindeman and Adriana were smug and comfortable in their little power roles. Certain they knew everything. Certain they were right.

That's what really bothered me.

I would never be like that. I'm certain of it.

Chapter Eleven
Getting the Goods

"Earthquakes just happen. Tornadoes just happen. Your tongue does not just happen to fall into some other girl's mouth."
~Gemma Halliday

Another late night ahead of me, I load the car with my equipment and supplies. Betsy has a full tank with plenty of oil and antifreeze. I put a cooler in the back with cans of Red Bull, two turkey sandwiches and a Ding Dong. (Turkey is good for you.) I have my cellphone, chargers and camera rig, including my night vision spotting scope. I also have my "spy toys," which I may actually be able to use. So far, I've been following Zoey Duncan for more than a week. She hasn't met up with Walter once. She's due.

Some private eyes use GPS trackers. I don't. If I'd been hired to find out if Walter was cheating, and both Kelly and Walter's name were on the car title, I could legally pop a tracking device on his car. Following him would be easy. But Kelly didn't necessarily hire me to catch Walter cheating, so I can't justify the tracker. In fact, I'm wondering how much I can bill Kelly Mason for the night hours I've been spending. I don't think she'd approve.

Besides, I'm not following Walter. I'm following Zoey. So, I won't touch her car.

For the first time, she heads out of town after work, taking I-25. Once again, she's got a heavy foot. I push Betsy to keep up. Driving south, I expect her to hit a motel in one of the small towns along the highway. She surprises me by going all the way to Denver. After turning off at the Speer Boulevard exit, I have to race to close the gap between our cars, lest I get stuck at a red light.

Big cities unnerve me. The streets are filled with garbage bags and refuse. Buildings rise like mountains of aluminum, concrete, and glass, bearing in on me as I drive. How do people live without actually touching the ground? Touching dirt? Maybe that's why the world has gone crazy. You can't live in glass and aluminum and stay sane.

My window is cracked open, and I smell rain and oil smoke. I check my rearview mirror to make sure Betsy's not spewing. She's old. You never know.

Zoey drives into downtown Denver, parking at a lot near the 16th Street Mall. I park in the same lot—I don't want to lose her. Out of the car and on foot, I have no such worries. She's wearing heels, and I'm wearing tennis shoes—they go with my ball cap.

She walks to the lit end of the pedestrian mall on 16th Street. Most of the mall and the side streets are shrouded in shadow.

The mall was a nice place, once. Back in the day, I'd drive to Denver for a weekend away. A nice hotel, dinner in a fine restaurant, a walk and late-night drinks. Plenty to enjoy. Bicycle rickshaws, street vendors, and buskers. Shuttle busses making a full circuit, packed with pedestrians. Quirky shops, from hatmakers to a model train store. Any kind of food you could imagine. Thai. Cajun. Tex-Mex. Indian. What my ex-wife used to call "Eye-talian."

Not now. The place is overrun by urban campers and bangers.

The dark expanse bothers me. You can see security floods on a few buildings down the way, but only one end of the mall—anchored by chain restaurants—is well-lit. I understand turning off the lights. Denver has budget constraints like every other city. In theory, you can't spend what you don't have. But downtown Denver is no longer safe. Fix blame however you like. The place reminds me of the parking lot by the Westbrook Community Center—just as dark and fifty times bigger. Even I don't feel safe. What the hell is Zoey thinking, walking down here alone?

And what does it say about the world when she can't reasonably do so?

As I trot to keep up with Zoey, who seems very adept in her heels, I manage to catch the edge of a small pile of feces. I stop and lift a leg, inspecting my shoe. An old black man nestles back in the entryway of a souvenir shop, the stub of a cigarette clamped in his teeth. He's grinning. "Watch out for that."

"Too late," I say, and move on. Ahead, a group of six blocks the walk, talking and smoking. Skinny white boys, not a single jacket among them, shivering in the night air. Zoey tries to pass, but one of the men sidesteps in front of her. Looking up, he sees me hurrying their way, and thinks better of whatever he had planned. He steps aside, and she slips by without a word.

I wind my way through the pack, a prickling sensation on the back of my neck. As I pass, one of the boys asks for change. I ignore him. The thought of getting hit from behind worries me, but I move ahead unharmed.

Meanwhile, Zoey reaches one of the chain restaurants, better known for desserts than for dinner food. I had a friend who worked there for a minute. The kitchen cuts every corner they can, using frozen, processed foods and microwave ovens. The lights are too bright, the music too loud. I wonder if I'm chasing wild geese again. Who would have a romantic dinner here?

The restaurant has one main room and two side rooms. The hostess tries to seat me at a table in one of the side rooms, but I ask for a spot in the main room, where Zoey sits, waiting. My table isn't close to hers, but that's okay. Half of the tables have been moved out in anticipation of the next health crisis, even though the last pandemic was a decade ago. The open space gives me clear line-of-sight to her table. I set my ball cap on the tabletop. Good manners. Besides, the camera in the cap works better when it's not on my head.

Then Walter shows up. I don't expect to be recognized, but I make sure I don't call attention to myself by staring. The couple greets without touching, and Walter sits down and goes straight to his menu. Could I be wrong about these two?

My waitress shows up, and I order a beer and a cheeseburger. She lists the beers on tap, then lists six kinds of cheese and four possible sides for my burger. All decisions made—the fate of the world seems to depend on my selection of pepper jack and onion rings—I sit back and watch.

Then I get lucky, so I activate the video cam.

My position across the room from the happy couple affords me a view of their feet under the table. Zoey has slipped her right foot out of her pump and placed her toes on his upper ankle.

Video doesn't lie. (Well, it does, but I don't use AI.) If I took a snap of the couple playing footsie, they might argue that the picture didn't provide context, the way social media likes to post pictures of politicians, one arm extended in a Nazi salute (which ought to convince politicians to keep their arms at their sides forever more). The bare foot would be harder to explain, but why risk it? Video provides context.

The same contextual problems hold true for phone messaging. Accessing someone's phone would be difficult for me without certain resources, though not impossible. But texts are easily explained as humor or harmless flirting.

It's not enough to gather sufficient proof to convince a spouse. You may have to convince a divorce court judge as well.

I need more evidence, so I linger over a gigantic slice of carrot cake, watching while Walter nibbles at his entrée. I swear to God, the man never takes a full bite. After my cake is gone, I order a second beer. "The cake was good, but beer is the real dessert," I say. "And bring me the tab." This last puts a smile on the waitress's face. Gives her hope that I'll vacate the table soon. Tab paid, I can follow if Walter and Zoey suddenly bolt for the door. Or, I can camp out, beer in hand.

As it turns out, I have fair warning for their exit. Walter makes a show out of paying—waving for the waitress and fishing a credit card out like it was made of platinum. When they finally leave, Walter plunges ahead while Zoey follows, arms folded in front of her. I leave half a beer behind and make for the door.

Outside, Zoey catches up to Walter, who doesn't seem angry. Just oblivious. She latches on to his arm, leaning into him as they walk. I pull out my cellphone, walking behind them as if I'm talking, snapping still shots and a short video clip. The cell camera has great resolution, so the other option stays on my head. Sometimes, a hat is just a hat.

Ahead, the same cluster of shivering boys blocks the way. Walter stops, then crosses the street to avoid them. I keep moving forward. If he's walking Zoey to her car, I want to get ahead of them. The boys stare sullenly as I approach. I continue my pretense of talking as I pass. "The suspect is in sight, Lieutenant," I say. "We'll take him at the next corner." The boys let me pass.

I turn left toward the parking lot, glancing back. The happy couple is following me, though they're not moving very fast. Walter walks like he eats.

I reach my car before they're on the lot, sliding into the front seat. I snap the cellphone into the bracket with the night vision monocular scope. By the time they reach Zoey's car, I'm ready.

And just like that, they kiss.

The embrace goes on forever, so I take bursts of still photos and a video clip. He gets a little handy with her, and I capture that as well. Nice to know that slow-moving Walter eventually gets busy. I was beginning to wonder what Zoey saw in him. Besides money and power, I mean.

I put the key in Betsy and she fires up on the first try. I pull out slowly, circling the row to avoid passing them directly. Out on the street, I turn myself toward home. Fumbling through my cassettes, most of them from the local pawn shop, I look for something sounding like triumph. *Also Spake Zarathustra* would be appropriate, but I left Strauss at home. The Ramones will have to do.

I have enough goods to present to Kelly Mason. The thought cheers me because it means I'll see her in a day or two. Then, I think about what the news will do to her. I think of what finding out about my wife's infidelity meant to me. Suddenly, *I Wanna Be Sedated* takes on new meaning.

If the night I caught my wife cheating wasn't the worst night of my life, it was in the top twenty, and those twenty nights were strung together, one after the other. For the first few weeks, I couldn't eat. I couldn't sleep. I couldn't shut off my brain. Was her infidelity a mistake? A test of my affections? Revenge for something I might have said or done? Anything but the end of us, right?

It was the end, of course.

How would Kelly Mason take the news? She was a cool one. Maybe, a cold one. Surely, she knew Walter was cheating. In my experience, if a man thinks his wife has strayed, he might be right or he might not. Fifty-fifty. But if a woman suspects cheating, she's usually right. Not because men are shits—which they are—but because women notice details. They sense things. They *know*.

Does Kelly Mason know her husband is a cheat? I think so. She's too smart *not* to know. And if she knows, then what's this job really about? Does she want to be able to say that the news was a surprise? Would that matter in court?

It might. Discovering his infidelity while attempting to protect him would certainly enhance her position as the wronged woman. Who knows? I don't know what kind of prenuptials they have.

I turn off the music, suddenly in the mood for silence.

What if Kelly hired me, knowing full well Walter was a cheat? That kind of manipulation fits the profile. Femme fatale, and all that crap. Too bad. She seemed nice.

In my business, you see the worst in people. You see their kids, who get torn apart by their parents' bullshit. Men beating their wives and girlfriends. Women cheating on the people who love them. Makes you want to stay single or get a dog. Or both. Truth is, caring about women hasn't worked out for me. And you can get used to being alone.

I roll down the window, but two minutes of cold wind convince me to roll it back up. Halfway home, I pull off on the frontage road and grab a turkey sandwich from the cooler. I just ate a burger, but I want something in my mouth besides sour. Halfway into the sandwich, I reach back again and grab a can of Red Bull. I'll need energy if I'm going to spend the night drinking.

Back home, I see my "residents' only" parking space is filled. Nice looking Subaru. Metallic green finish. I'm jealous. I'm also tired of students taking my parking spot.

I drive three blocks east, park Betsy where she won't be bothered and head for Old Town. The closest alcohol is a martini bar—upscale place with low lighting and high prices. I walk another hundred feet and step into the Thirsty Dog, a beer and shot joint. Lo and behold—Billotte spots me from behind the bar.

He has a new job.

The place is nearly empty, so I grab a stool in the middle of the bar. He comes over, grinning, wearing a lime green vest and a red bow tie. His thin brown hair is combed straight across the top of his head, from left to right. He looks like an organ grinder. I wonder if he has a monkey under the counter.

"Slag! Welcome to my new home. What can I get you? It's on the house."

"Bullshit. You're new here. You need to charge me." I shake my head. "You're a waiter. Since when do you sling drinks?"

"I can pull a tap, same as you. Beer and a shot for you?"

I nod.

"What are you up to? Working a case?"

I give him a brief rundown on my visit to Denver. I add a line or two about how sad it is that somebody like Kelly Mason is going to face unwelcome news. By the time I'm finished blabbing, I'm on my second round. The liquor is going down super-smooth, which is dangerous. I pause long enough to consider my mood. Why does the evening's business, clearly successful, leave me drinking in the kind of bar that thinks hiring Bobby Billotte is a good idea?

Meanwhile, Billotte mixes a shot for a new customer. I recognize him as a cook from one of the nearby restaurants. Balding, sway-backed, and thin as hell, already old at thirty-plus, he knocks back the shot and wipes his mouth with the sleeve of his Bears jersey. He turns right, nods at me, then turns back to his empty glass.

I look up. The bar walls are pine, covered in memorabilia, most of it nailed or screwed into the wall above where anyone can reach it. Probably for the best. You never know when somebody's going to rip an old highway yield sign off the wall and bash someone's head with it.

My cellphone vibrates in my pocket. I'm inclined to ignore it, having already decided I'm going to close this bar. Force of habit compels me. I answer without checking the number.

"Mark?"

I look down at my cell, incredulous.

"Mark?"

"What?" I ask. My voice is suddenly dry.

"Can you hear me?" The television over the bar is on, and the house speakers are blaring a Bachman-Turner Overdrive song. I motion Bobby over and point at my cellphone. "I have to take this outside," I say. "I'll be back. I won't run out on you."

"Better not," Bobby says. "I need you to pay for those drinks I tried to give you for free."

"Just a minute," I say into the phone. Then I give Billotte the finger and head outside. A cold breeze makes my spine stiffen. I step into the alley beside the bar and lean against the wall. "Can you hear me now?"

"Yes, that's better."

"What's up?" My voice sounds casual, like I'm not shaking. Like I'm not talking to my ex-wife for the first time in two years.

"They let me go at work."

"Sorry to hear that."

"Yeah," she says with a sad stutter of a laugh.

"Is what's-his-name still working?"

"I don't know. I guess so. I haven't talked to him recently."

I use the subsequent silence to sort through the thought-tornado ripping up the inside of my head. Is she angling to come home? Would I even want her back? I hope not.

No. She doesn't like dogs.

"I need to ask you for a loan. Otherwise, I'm going to be on the street at the end of the month."

A car comes crawling past. Dark windows. Like in a gangster movie. I'm grateful. I need the distraction. I clear my throat. "Why me? What about your folks?"

"Dad's sick. They're trying to make ends meet."

"You could move home. It's not ideal, but—"

Her voice shifts, and my old friend—her sarcasm—comes roaring back. "What? Move into the rest home with him?"

"Rest home?"

"Mom and Dad moved into managed care last year."

"Oh," I say. "I didn't know."

Silence. Then, "You're my last chance."

"Flattering."

She utters another bitter laugh. "I'm trying to tell you I wouldn't make this call unless you were my last hope. I wouldn't do that to you."

Some impositions are apparently off the table.

The wind whips up a little, like a front moving in. Not much traffic on the street, which surprises me. A candy wrapper rolls past, headed west toward Main Street. I clear my throat. "How much do you need?"

She mentions an amount. "That gets me through the month. I don't know what I'm going to do about next month yet."

"Are you working?"

"No, I just told you. They let me go. Otherwise, I wouldn't have to call." She seems to understand that her voice has a shrill edge to it, because when she speaks again, she manages a softer tone. "The shop closed. People aren't buying flowers, not in this economy. Unemployment won't cover all my bills, and anyway, it will run out."

"You might have to switch professions."

"You think?" The shrill is back.

"You need more than a quick fix. Remember my restaurant job? The one you never liked? Lucky I kept it. It's enough to give you a loan." I pause. "But it's not enough to keep both of us floating."

"I understand," she promises. I imagine her nodding, her brown curls swaying with the motion, like when she said, "Of course our marriage is still important to me."

"Same address? I'll mail a check."

"Don't," she says. "It takes two weeks for a letter to get through the Post Office. Can you send me money online?"

Yes, I can. I promise to send, first thing in the morning.

"Thank you." A pause. "I feel so empty. I miss my job. I miss caring for them. Arranging them. Everything. Flowers, I mean." As an afterthought, she asks, "How are you doing?"

If she'd started with that, I'd have told her to cut the small talk and get to the point. Ending with that seems like checking a box on the list of good manners. She can't win. "I'm fine," I say. Lies are my friend.

She knows the call is almost over. "You won't forget, will you?"

"One call in two years? No, I won't forget."

"I didn't think you wanted me to call."

"I didn't." Hanging up, I go back inside the bar. Billotte asks, "Everything okay?"

I nod and point to the empty glassware in front of me. "Hit me."

"Done."

I sag in my seat and try to think of something to say that will properly express the feelings surging through me. "Love is an onion." Cliché. "Love is blind." Thanks Billy Shakes. As for me, I got nothing.

Billotte slides a beer my way, and it's halfway down my throat before he can pour my shot.

"You upset about something?" he asks.

"The impossibility of maintaining a long-term relationship," I mutter.

He smiles and taps the bar with a fingertip. "That's a *good* thing."

Chapter Twelve
Second Warning

"There's a difference between violence and senseless violence."
~DMX

I wake up around noon, mouth open and gritty, like I've been chewing drywall. I'm supposed to meet Lee and Manny at the Community Center at one, so I send some cash to the ex over the phone, walk Sasha, and grab a cup of coffee on the way to my car. But when I reach my parking spot, the car is gone. I stare at the empty spot with what must be a stupid, vacant look on my face. Was my car stolen?

No, I drank last night. I left Betsy blocks away and never went back for her. A tiny wave of relief battles with irritation at the time I am wasting. I arrive at the center ten minutes late.

Lee wants to spar first. Lee *always* wants to go first. He squares off against me, ducking and swooping like a City Park goose, gloves in front of his face. He draws his shoulder back and lets a jab fly. I slip the jab and tap him in the chest. He flops back, squares up, and moves in again.

This is my warmup. Manny stands to the side, watching, no discernable expression on his face. But his gaze is locked on me, and I know he's thinking about ways to attack.

After three minutes, we break. I'm puffing. Lee is trying not to. Manuel is ready to go.

"Give me a second," I say, hands on my knees. I know I look old. I don't mind. Gives me an edge. Youth is forever overconfident. I take a last deep breath, and wave Manny forward.

"Nah, let me box Manny," Lee says. He rolls his shoulders in a circular motion, shrugging and grinning like he's just given this old man a standing eight. "I'll kick his ass for you, Slag."

Manny tilts his head, the corners of his mouth twitching.

"God damn it, Lee. We're supposed to be sparring. This isn't Caesar's Palace."

"Where?" Lee seems genuinely confused.

I sigh. "Las Vegas. Back in the day, they used to hold championship bouts there."

"Back in the day?" Lee says. "Greek days or Roman days?"

Manny lets a laugh escape his lips, then buries his face in his forearm, shaking his head.

"Caesar's Palace sounds Roman to me," Lee continues. He's on a roll. "Tell me something—did you wear a toga back then?"

"A torn one. Torn all to hell. They called me Euripides."

Manny bursts out laughing. Lee shakes his head. "What?"

"It's a joke," I tell him. "Euripides was a Greek playwright."

Lee looks incredulous. Manny is still laughing, and Lee turns to him. "You didn't know that. Don't tell me you knew that because you didn't."

"Okay, I won't tell you." Manny steps back as if he's done talking and says, "They criticized his plays for portraying slaves as intelligent."

"Who is *they*?"

Manny smiles. "The people at Caesar's Palace."

Now I'm bent over with laughter, and Manny can't keep a straight face.

"Fuck you guys," Lee says, waving them off. "Are we gonna box, or what?"

We box. Six rounds total. If you want to know what that's like, run bleacher steps at top speed for three minutes. Then walk, still climbing steps, until the next round starts. By the time we finish, my hoodie is soaked in sweat. My right shoulder hurts from swinging and missing Manny, who can bob and weave like a pro. And I have a swollen lip where Manny popped me with that sneaky left hook of his, though Lee thinks he did it with a right cross. "Get some ice on that, old man," Lee tells me as we clean up, ready to leave.

"Thanks, Doctor Lee," I tell him.

After Lee is gone, I have to ask. "You know Euripides?"

"Of course," he says, stuffing his towel into his gym bag. "My mother made us read all the classics."

"Smart mom," I say. "You been to college?"

He shakes his head. "Gotta work."

"What do you do?"

"Boilermaker."

I say, "Guess you don't mean the drink." I am, after all, a bartender.

He smiles. "I install and repair boilers and other closed vats. Copper pipes and valves."

"How did you get into that?"

"My mother arranged an apprenticeship with my uncle."

"You make good money?"

The tight-lipped smile tells me it's none of my business.

"Well, hell, you're full of surprises."

"You don't think Mexicans read the classics?"

"I didn't think Mexicans handled water pipes. Meth pipes, maybe."

Manuel bursts out laughing again. "You're fast, Slag. Fast hands, fast mouth. That ever get you in trouble?"

"Every day," I say. We bump fists, and he heads out. I watch him walk down the hall, a bounce in his step like he hadn't even broken a sweat. Good kid. Smart. The sort of person who deserves to have a good life. I feel a sudden knot in the pit of my stomach. I know there are two separate threads to the knot. I worry for the future and regret the past.

His future. My past.

As I stand considering, my sore shoulder pressed to the wall, Santiago Alvarez comes striding past, his attention on the men's room door. He goes in, and suddenly, I have an opportunity to talk to him alone. No homies.

I check the hallway in both directions. No one else coming. I go inside. Santiago stands at a urinal, staring at the wall in front of him.

"Zip up," I tell him.

"What?" He stares at me, as if he's trying to figure out who I am.

"Zip it up," I tell him. "We're going to have a talk."

"Fuck you," he says, but he's zipping. I start toward him, and he moves, hand to pocket. The knife is out before I even realize what he's doing.

Boxing is an instinctive sport. You train yourself to move a certain way, throw thousands of punches, and move your feet and head until every move is natural. In the ring, you don't have time to consider anything. You look for openings, but if you stop to think, "He dropped his guard—I should throw an uppercut," your chance is gone, and you'll end up on your back.

Santiago closes the gap between us, and I react. Three seconds later, Santi's head bounces off the floor tile and the knife tumbles away. He blinks and reaches out to grab the weapon. I stomp on his hand.

I give him credit. He doesn't scream.

I kick the knife into a bathroom stall. He starts to get up but thinks better of it. "If you get up, I'll put you in the hospital. Just stay there on the floor and listen."

His eyes glaze with pain. He lies still, staring at the knife ten feet away.

"I told you to leave Minnie alone," I say. "But you went to see her."

"Fuck you."

"Don't talk," I say. "Shut up and listen."

His eyes are as red as poppies.

"You'll go see Minnie again. You're too stupid not to. And when you do, I'm going to find you and beat you. I will make you bleed inside. You'll wake up every night, weeping, wishing you'd been smarter. I'm telling you how it's going to be because you're too stupid to just stay away."

"You're dead," he says. I look into his eyes, and I believe.

So, I kick him. I feel ribs snap, and this time, he gasps.

"You sad, stupid little man. Remember what's coming." I back away. He immediately begins crab-crawling toward the knife, groaning with the effort. I shake my head and leave.

The hallway is still empty.

* * * * *

Santiago's eyes, red as poppies.

My ex-wife was a florist. With the possible exception of infidelity, flowers were her life's passion. She knew the story and symbolism behind every flower. And poppies were the gateway to her passion.

Her great-great-grandfather Jonas fought in World War One. He took a piece of shrapnel in the shoulder during the Battle of Belleau Wood, which rendered his arm mostly useless for the rest of his life. In his later years, he doted on his great-great-granddaughter because she listened to his war stories long after the rest of the family relegated him to the back corner of family gatherings.

The old man tended poppies in his garden at home. Pretty flowers, right? I'm not talking about the poppies used to extract opium. I'm talking about red poppies. Field poppies.

One of the old man's stories changed the direction of a young girl's life. "The Germans shelled a cornfield for three days," he'd explain each time he retold the tale. "They turned it into a mass of mud and craters—everything burned or buried. The Americans held the tree line behind the field, and that's where we stayed, dug into holes, waiting. The Great War was like that. Men gathered in huge groups, facing each other for weeks before one side or the other decided to commit suicide by closing the gap. All for tiny patches of land like the cornfield.

"Rumor had it, we were going to mount an assault, which frightened me to the bone. I thought I was going to die in that field. I surely did. But it never happened. Days went by. Then weeks. One night, the Germans pulled back, trying to consolidate their lines. This was near the end of the war, you see, and they were just about spent.

"Time came to cross the field. We were all feeling grateful to pick our way over the crater holes, rather than run over them with bullets flying. I expected the field to look like the surface of the moon. But that's not what I found."

"Poppies!" my future ex-wife would say, forever delighted by the idea.

"Poppies," he'd agree. "Clumps of red flowers covering the carnage like nature's blanket. The more scarred the land, the more poppies I found. Those swatches of red were the most beautiful thing I'd ever seen. We were mesmerized."

Field poppies germinate when soil is disturbed. That's why you find them in ploughed fields—or land blown to hell by artillery shells. After the war, red poppies served as a reminder for the sacrifice so many men made. Others regarded poppies as a symbol of war and its glorification and came to hate the flower.

I liked the history behind the old man's story. My ex-wife liked flowers and the stories behind them. Originally from Mesopotamia, red poppy seeds can lay dormant for 100 years before springing to life, germinating best in disturbed soil. As she grew older, she learned the stories behind other flowers, but she kept a special place in her heart for the red bloom that reminded her of her great-grandfather and how life could spring from death.

Symbolism is personal. I hate poppies. Among other things, I link them to death, whether on a battlefield in Europe or in the bloodshot eyes of a thug who would have sliced me open if he'd had the chance, spilling my blood over the tiles of a public restroom floor.

I also link them to my cheating ex-wife. I imagine her coloring the flowers red with my heart's blood.

To hell with poppies. And to hell with war, and to hell with my ex-wife.

Heading home, I make plans to spend time with Sasha. I will walk her and cook something fresh on the hot plate. Maybe a chicken breast. Sasha loves chicken. I don't mind spoiling her.

You can judge a person by how they treat animals, right?

I think about poppies and war and Santiago. I picture him lying there on the tile, red-eyed and helpless. I wonder about the line between self-defense and unjustifiable violence. In war, people shoot at you. You shoot at them. You don't choose to be there unless you're one of the numbskulls who volunteers.

Santiago came at me with a knife. Self-defense, though you *could* argue that you shouldn't call somebody out in the bathroom. Maybe the knife was *his* self-defense. Of course, I'd never have confronted him if he hadn't threatened Minnie. And he might have left her alone if I hadn't opened my mouth.

I stop still, hands jammed in my pockets.

Fuck that noise. The son of a bitch came at me with a knife. Hitting him and watching his head bounce on the tile was pure joy. I loved stepping on the bastard's hand, too. I enjoyed snapping his ribs.

As for the right or wrong of it, I'll think about that later.

Chapter Thirteen
The Turn

"Writers are always writing about infidelity. It's so dramatic. The wickedness of it, the secrecy, the complications, the finding that you thought you were one person but you're also this other person. The innocent life and the guilty life. My God, it's just full of stuff for a writer. I doubt it will ever go out of fashion."
~Alice Munro

I have a lunch meeting with Kelly Mason, so instead of pushing my hair around and splashing my face, I go to the community center for a shower. I'm a little concerned about crossing paths with Santiago or his homies, but that's bound to happen sooner or later. I'll put on a stone face and see what that gets me. We may just ignore each other from here on out, and that will be fine with me.

My one moment of concern comes when I'm in the center's shower room. I can understand the vulnerability jail inmates feel. I give everyone around me a second and third look, waiting for an attack that never comes. I'm especially careful when walking out.

The locker room smells of sweat, anti-fungal sprays and cologne. I plan lunch as I dress. Telling someone their husband is a cheat is dicey at best. I'd like to minimize Kelly's humiliation. Is that possible? I don't think so. A cheating spouse sends the message that you don't measure up. You're not attractive enough to keep the relationship alive. The person your spouse cheats with may be shit, but at least they're not dull or ugly. Escargot wins, oatmeal loses.

I brush my teeth at one of the sinks. Then, I change into button-down shirt and dress slacks. I do own a tie. One. I didn't bring it.

On my way back to the center of town, I consider how I will break the news to Kelly about her husband. Approach the disclosure with a cavalier attitude, and somebody's going to get hurt. Physically.

Tell a man his wife is cheating, and he'll sit there, dumbfounded. When he goes home, he might pack his bags. He might beat her. He might even go after the man she's cheating with. Some rough-cut bastards do nothing. Some quiet sorts go ballistic. You just can't tell.

Tell a woman her husband is cheating, and she's likely to go home and confront him on the spot. Then the husband will come looking for the investigator.

Because I can be ham-fisted, I practice my approach.

I have hard news for you, Mrs. Mason. I need you to steel yourself. Your husband has not been faithful.

Mrs. Mason, I have bad news. This is going to hurt, and I'm sorry about that. Your husband has been unfaithful. I want you to know you're not alone in this. Statistics say up to seventy percent of all marriages suffer infidelity from one partner or the other.

Mrs. Mason, your husband is having an affair. Understand, please, this isn't necessarily the death knell for your marriage. Many couples find they can communicate best when there are no more secrets. If you can begin communicating, the truth can mean a fresh start for both of you.

Or.

I am sorry to be the one to tell you this, Kelly. Your husband is having an affair. Frankly, I'm stunned. The man doesn't deserve you. My opinion.

By the time I reach the Mexican food place, I'm sweating like a kid in his first tux. I'm a half hour early, planning to arrive before her, but she's already at a table, sipping sweet tea.

The manila envelope in my hand has still photos. The videos I took are on my cellphone in case she wants to watch. She looks up, recognizes me, and smiles. The smile does me in. Suddenly, I'm not ready for this meeting.

A sinking feeling anchors me to the floor, ten feet away from the booth where she sits. I don't want to be the one to give her the bad news. I don't want to be this woman's agent of pain.

She tilts her head. I'm still locked in place.

"Are you all right?" she asks. The concern seems real.

I sit down. She's wearing a blue sweater. It's not as tight as it might be. Her hair is pinned up, as usual.

Our waitress, someone new, comes to the table. I order a salad, and Kelly does the same. After the waitress leaves, I place the envelope on the tabletop and slide it over to her. "I'm sorry," I say. Then, silence.

Apparently, I'm a man of few words.

She stares at the envelope for a long time before opening it. She removes the photos and looks at them one by one, shuffling the top photo to the back of the stack; cycling through until she's viewed them all. She sets the pile on top of the envelope and stares at it, her mouth drawn down at the corners.

"Are you all right?" I ask.

She covers her mouth with her hand and blinks. I see tears.

"I can give you a moment."

"Thank you," she says. Her voice carries a tremor. I expect her to go to the restroom, but instead, she takes a sip of tea and sits. When the waitress arrives to take our orders, she speaks softly—only a whisper. After a while, she sighs, and looks up at me.

"This gal," I say, nodding at the pile of photos, "is who they're blackmailing your husband with."

"What do they want? Do you know?"

"I'm not certain. But I suspect it has something to do with Maurice Brown's restaurant, Downtown Chicken. Your husband's office is at odds with the restaurant—"

"I told *you* that." Her voice carries a hint of challenge, as if the only things I know are the things she told me in the first interview. As if I've been fooling around instead of investigating.

"I believe the city wants the restaurant closed so it can acquire the property for a downtown community center."

"Why would you think that?"

"I saw blueprints. The project is already in the works."

Her mouth opens in surprise. She sits back, her gaze unfocused. After a moment, she asks, "Are you saying my husband is trying to shut the restaurant down to make room for the center?"

I shrug. "I don't know what your husband's role is. He may just be trying to do his job. But somebody either wants the restaurant closed, and is pressuring him to do so, or wants the restaurant to stay open, and is pressuring him to back off." I pause. "If Mo Brown is behind this, then he's trying to save his restaurant. He seems to have identified your husband as the enemy. I have a witness who said—"

"Are you saying my husband is part of some kind of conspiracy?"

"As I told you, I don't know your husband's role."

Her lips press into a thin line. She glances at the photos again, and says, "These might not mean what they appear to mean. The woman might be a business associate. The angle might make things look worse than they are."

I take my cellphone from my back pocket and set it on the table. "I have video."

Her gaze narrows and her lips purse. I hit the icon on my cell to call up a video, but she waves me off. "I don't need to see. I'll take your word."

"All right."

She places a hand on the top photo. "You've been following him, obviously. How much did this cost me?"

"Nothing," I say. The word is out of my mouth before I can even think. I'd debated how much I could charge her, being as proof of her husband's infidelity was not what I was hired to find. According to my mouth, which is currently working independent of my mind, I'm not charging her at all. "It was important to know what your husband was being threatened with. You were concerned they might hurt him. That doesn't appear to be the case. That's a good thing, right? As for the photos, most clients won't believe something like this unless I can prove it. But I didn't charge you for them."

She stares at me. "Why not?"

"I mean, I was hired to find out who was threatening your husband. So, I followed him, and this is what I found. That's legit. I was pretty sure this is what was going on, and I wanted to verify it. Some of that was personal curiosity." Words spill out of me like a bathtub overflowing. Or a toilet. I can't shut up. Where is the man of few words when I need him? "I don't sleep, anyway, so the extra time is on the house. Pro bono."

"Please stop," she says.

So, we sit, silent. The waitress delivers our salads, but neither of us picks up a fork.

Kelly clears her throat. "Have you been following me as well?"

"No."

"Really? Because—"

"I wouldn't do that." My voice thickens. I no longer want to be here. "Look, I'm sorry about this." I tap the pile of photos. "But you hired me to find out the truth. Sometimes, the truth sucks. But you have options. A lot of couples find that with secrets out in the open—"

"I recognize the pitch, Mr. Ferguson. My husband and I have been through counseling."

My turn to stare.

"This isn't the first transgression." Her face is aging in front of me, or maybe I'm taking a closer look. Her forehead creases with worry lines, or maybe lines of sorrow. Her eyes are reddened. I turn away.

I've made a mess of this meeting. What was I thinking?

I know the answer to that question, of course. But I won't sort through the tangled thoughts that lead a man whose marriage ended in infidelity to look forward to sharing the same deep-seated pain with someone else.

After another long silence, made less painful by the arrival of our food, she says, "Tell me about the blueprint."

"Plans for remodel of the restaurant and some neighboring shops. Turn the whole thing, upstairs and down, into a community center."

"How can you be sure?"

"The address was on the blueprint."

"What's upstairs? Now, I mean."

"Offices. Storage. Once in a while, a business sublets a room up there, but it's pretty rough. They'll probably just knock down walls and turn it into a workout area."

Kelly shifts in her seat, careful not to squeak the vinyl seat beneath her. She does not meet my gaze. "Where did you see this blueprint?"

"On the desk of Armando de San Martín."

Her eyes widen. "Does he know you saw it?"

"We were in the office together, but he would have no reason to think I had any interest in the blueprint. As it was, I was only able to glance."

"And you're sure he won't connect you with my husband?"

"We discussed the possibility of a new community center in the context of getting space for the boxers who spar there. To him, I'm just a guy who hits the heavy bag."

She sits back, considering what I'd said. She starts to ask another question, then stops, shaking her head. Glancing down, she sees her untouched salad and pushes it aside. I do the same, and her frown deepens. "You are welcome to eat, Mr. Ferguson. I've lost my appetite."

"I understand. I do."

She looks away. "Really?"

"My wife," I say, and suddenly, I have nothing to add.

"Then I'm sorry for you as well." Her voice is back in control. "This is where someone well-intentioned would quote a statistic about how common infidelity is. As if that would make *anyone* feel better."

"No comfort there," I agree.

"What about the other names on the list?"

"I spoke to both the professor and your husband's assistant."

"You didn't explain too much, I hope."

"Of course not. Both parties believe I'm a freelance writer doing an article on Health and Environment."

"And what are your thoughts about them?"

"I don't believe either one is involved. Your husband's assistant is a rather enthusiastic supporter of your husband's work." Kelly nods. "As for the professor, I don't think he has the wherewithal to threaten anyone."

"Wherewithal?" A hint of her smile is back, if only for a moment.

"He's a little man."

Kelly reflects on this and nods. "I hope you looked beyond my list for other possibilities."

I feel a moment of panic, but then I remember my initial searches. "I've been through his social media, and it's squeaky clean. All business. No funny business. I wonder if he's got someone making his posts for him. Keep him out of trouble."

Kelly whispers something to herself. I think she said, "Naomi."

"I also traced all the people who posted comments, especially the angry ones. I didn't find much. Your husband is surprisingly popular for a government official."

"That's because he's a good man," she says. When I don't answer, she locks her gaze onto mine and continues. "People make mistakes. But Walter takes civil service to heart. He wouldn't do the things you might be suspecting him of." She tilts her head again, and her open expression reminds me of Sasha.

I'm tempted to ask something smarmy, like, "What do you think I suspect him of?" But this isn't a game. Instead, I ask something that matters. "Do you want me to stop looking?"

We have endured several silences, but the one that follows is the longest yet. I begin to wonder if I imagined asking a question.

"No, Mr. Ferguson," she finally says. "I trust my husband. . . in certain arenas. But if I'm wrong, and he's involved in dirty business, I suppose I need to know. Please continue your investigation. Do you need additional funds?"

"No. I'll let you know if the money runs out."

The waitress passes by, her hands full of empty plates. She notices the lettuce in Kelly's salad is safe from consumption. My burrito thing has one bite gone. "Was there something wrong with your lunches?"

"No, they're fine," I say.

"I can get you something different if you don't like them."

"Really, they're fine."

Kelly sits, silent.

The waitress, a chunky brunette with reddened cheeks, says, "But you haven't touched a single bite!" She's concerned, but her voice seems strident. Besides, I had indeed taken a bite.

I try a joke, which is almost never a good idea. "I'm trying to diet. I hate burritos, so I order them and stare at them with disdain."

Her forced smile turns to a frown, as if I've made fun of her. I didn't, not intentionally. I'm just horribly, horribly uncomfortable. The waitress scurries off to trade whispers with the manager, who nods. To my dismay, she returns to the table, her arms folded in front of her. "We're sorry you didn't enjoy your meal. We're going to comp both entrees. We hope you'll give us another try."

Kelly intervenes. "We will. Thank you so much for your kindness," and like magic, the waitress is happy again. I drop a Tubman on the table anyway. The girl can keep it as a tip.

As I rise to leave, Kelly asks me to wait. "I do have one more thing I want to say." I sit back down. She pushes the pile of photos at me. "Please take these with you." I nod, and she continues. "My husband is a *good* man." Her gaze flicks back to the photos for an instant. "Everyone falls short of who they ought to be. *Everyone.* But I know him, and his heart is good. He cares about his job and the people he serves. And I know he loves me.

"I suspect you see people at their worst. That might color how you see the world, and you might be inclined to concentrate on finding out what Walter has done wrong. I'm asking you to give equal time to proving his innocence. Equal time because I believe he *is* a good man. If, when we're done, you believe that, too, then I'll know I'm not being foolish."

I'm touched, and I promise to keep an open mind. That promise stays with me as I walk out into the sun, heading down Main Street and into Old Town Plaza, a cool breeze pushing me past the fountain and the sculptures and the fading flower beds. But by the time I reach the door to my apartment building, I wonder once more if I'm being played.

Could someone love someone else so selflessly as to forgive the unforgiveable? To offer support to the unsupportable? Does that kind of love exist?

Long odds, indeed.

Chapter Fourteen
Closing Time

"Many troubled Midwestern towns are grasping for ways to fend off decline and, in some cases, extinction."
~Stephen Kinzer

I spend the rest of the week chasing geese again. Not those squawkers in City Park. The kind of geese that look like clues until you get close and realize that they are, in fact, mile markers on the road to wasted time. When my weekly shift at Wesley's rolls around, I'm anxious to start pouring drinks for several reasons, not the least of which involves money.

Billotte shows up, having not had his fill of my bullshit the night before. We'd gone out drinking, yet here he was at my bar, a shot of Smirnoff's in front of him. "They didn't need you at your place tonight?" I ask.

"I haven't been there long enough to pull a Friday or Saturday shift. Soon, though. The night guy is raiding the till, and he's not going to last."

"You suspect that, or know it for a fact?"

"I watched him. He's not very good."

"Not if you caught him," I say.

Billotte pretends not to be amused.

Business is surprisingly good, which cheers me up. Between the servers and the customers at the bar, I keep moving. I know a lot of the regulars and remember what they drink. That saves me time. The day shift did a lousy job cleaning up. The floor mats are covered in spilled beer, drink straws, and wet napkins. I don't have time to clean up now, so I'm going to have a mess at the end of the night. But with the prospect of a good night, the mats are a minor irritation.

After dinner, the rush peaks and begins to taper off, Lloyd walks in. I'd wondered if I'd see him again any time soon. He grabs a seat to the left of Billotte and gives me a little wave. I set a shot glass on the bar top, fill it with vodka, and slide it over.

"I thought that was mine," Billotte says.

"I'm pacing you," I explain. "Ten minutes."

"What, are you my Mom now?"

"Parole officer," I say. Lloyd is sipping, and he chokes on my joke.

"How's work?" I ask him.

Lloyd waits a moment before answering, the corners of his mouth turned down. "Things are getting tense," he said. No elaboration. I pour him another shot. "Mo is going off his rocker, if you know what I mean."

"Tell me," I say. Billotte is silent, listening.

"They had another meeting with the health inspector this week. Mo had us cleaning all week, which is fucked up, because the building is a mess. We're just scrubbing the paint off the walls at this point." He drank half of his shot. Seeing my confused expression, he explains, "I'm trying to slow down."

"See?" I tell Billotte. "Pace yourself."

Billotte is silent.

"So, how did Mo handle the inspection?"

Lloyd purses his lips and shakes his head. Then he drinks the other half shot. He rubs his chin, which is covered in shaving bumps.

I've lingered long enough, so I slide down the bar, selling more liquor. When I get back, both Billotte and Lloyd have pushed empties to my side of the bar top. I refill the glasses.

"So anyway," Lloyd is saying to Billotte, "Mo fills up one of those twenty-five-ounce mugs with beer after lunch, walks into the office, and closes the door."

"Sounds like a happy ending," I say.

"Not hardly," Lloyd says. "Mo doesn't drink."

"Food service is a rough business," Billotte says. "Drive you to despair." He downs his shot.

"Owning any business is scary," I say.

Lloyd's head bobs up and down. "True dat. The boys upstairs have been freaking out."

"Boys upstairs?"

"The other owners," Lloyd explains.

"I thought Mo was the owner."

"One of them. The others have an office upstairs. They don't usually come around, but this week, they've been in the kitchen more than I have." His face draws down, like the human version of a basset hound. "I hate those guys." He pushes his nose to the side. Either they smell, or he's saying they're wise guys.

A server waves a drink ticket at the far end of the bar. Otherwise, I'd stay and listen. By the time I return, the conversation has moved on to the attributes of the various women they've worked with. Billotte nods at his empty glass.

"Still pacing," I say. I turn back to Lloyd. "I'm curious. How does Mo get along with the other owners?"

"Not well, these days. They blame him for the problems we're having with the city."

"Are they white? The other owners?"

"Does the Pope shit in the woods?" Lloyd hiccups. I splash bitters on a lime wedge and hand it to him.

"Mo is the front man?"

Lloyd nods while sucking on the lime. He makes a sour face. "Damn! That's nasty."

"People die from the hiccups," I remind him. "I may have just saved your life." Not that Lloyd's going to die, but he *is* prone to hiccups. For whatever reason, the lime and bitters get rid of them.

Looking up, I see Warren, back to the far wall, staring at me, his hairy arms crossed over his chest. The light on the wall sconce above him shines off his bald head. Just as I'm wondering if he's ever considered having some of his arm hair transplanted up on top, he unfolds and walks over. Putting one hand on Billotte's shoulder and the other on Lloyd's, he asks, "Are either of these gentlemen actually paying for their drinks?"

"What?" I must have misheard.

"I'm wondering if these guys are paying, or if you're just running up tips for yourself."

Lloyd's face goes as pale as his pigment will allow. Billotte's face is red as a tomato.

"Bad joke, Warren," I manage.

Warren points a finger at me. "See me after work."

"Count on it," I tell him.

When the owner leaves, Lloyd shakes his head, his mouth open.

"I'm sorry for that," I say. My voice is shaking. Lloyd has had two shitty visits in a row. He's going to stop coming here. I don't blame him. Meanwhile, Billotte sits and steams. His thin brown hair falls in front of his face, but he doesn't bother to brush it aside. His hands grip the edge of the bar top.

I refill their glasses. "*These* shots are on the house," I tell them. "Fuck that guy."

* * * * *

Every bartender on the planet gives out free drinks. Some overdo it. I actually knew a bartender who paid for a customer's drink rather than comp it. He didn't last long in the business.

Some bars have a set policy. Wesley's doesn't. When I first started behind the bar, I asked his thoughts about comp drinks. Warren said, "Yeah, you can comp a drink for a good customer. Just don't give away the house." So, yes, I pour free drinks. But I don't overdo it. If somebody comes in feeling entitled, they get nothing. I once had a guy order a rum and coke and say, "Hit me heavy. I'm a good tipper." I measured his shot like the rum bottle was Fort Knox. Guys who tie the tip to the pour are blowhards.

Lloyd has been coming in at least once a week for a year, serving up a big slice of his tiny kitchen paycheck to Warren on a regular basis. He's never asked for anything free. For him, I'll comp a drink or three. Call it a perk of the business, for a cook with damned few perks in his life. Am I running up my tip? *A tip from a cook?* Don't be an idiot.

After the bar closes, I finish cleaning up. As predicted, the floor mats are a disaster. I take them back, one at a time, and hose them off in the dish pit. When I'm finished, I sit on a barstool and wait. Warren hasn't come out for his usual beers. He's probably nursing a liquor bottle in the office, hoping I'll go home. He never even came for the cash tray. He sent one of the servers to fetch it.

I am probably out of a job, which worries me. I have savings. I won't be on the street—not until they start remodeling the apartments. But I've worked here for years, and this strikes me as a terrible way to go out.

When I get tired of waiting, which happens pretty quick, I head to the back of the restaurant, through the kitchen and down the hall where the employee bathrooms are. Warren's office door is closed. I knock. No immediate answer, so I knock again.

He jerks open the door, a wild look on his face. "What?" he demands.

"Time to talk," I tell him.

"I'm busy." He starts to close the door. My foot won't let him.

"What happened tonight was unacceptable." I push my way into the office and lay two drink tickets on the desk. "These are the tickets for the two customers you insulted. I marked the comp drinks—two each—on the tickets. I gave out a total of nine free drinks tonight. Three of them went to the art gallery woman—the one you've been hitting on."

Warren glances at the tickets. "Great. I'm glad to see you went back and charged them something."

I square up. "You're coming damned close to calling me a thief, and you *know* better. At least you should, being as I've been working your bar for years." His face is a cipher. If he clipped those eyebrows, I might be able to read an expression. "That was not like you, Warren. What's up?"

"Nothing's up."

"Bullshit. I know you, boss, and that wasn't you. You'd never do something like that."

His lower lip perches on top his upper lip, and for a moment, I think the little guy is going to reach up and pop me in the chest. Then, the lip starts to quiver. "I'm closing down," he says.

"What?"

"I'm shutting the place down. Can't keep it going anymore. We're going under."

"I don't understand. We do good business—"

"Taxes," he says, spitting the word. "I'm behind on payroll taxes. They keep raising them. Now, they're sending me registered mail. Going to attach my accounts."

"How'd you get behind?" I'm numb, so I'm asking numbskull questions.

"In the old days, we'd pack people in here. Can't do it anymore. Sales have been down, what with all the shit they let go on downtown. I got behind, and I can't catch up, not with the penalties and interest. Not with half a restaurant. I thought summer sales would bail me out, but now it's fall, and I'm further behind than I was three months ago. I did the books today, and I can make payroll this week. Barely. Next week? I don't think so."

I plunk down in the chair opposite Warren's desk. He circles the desk and sits, grabbing the bottle I knew he had. Top shelf whiskey. No glass.

The office is tiny. Located in the back, near the restrooms, the office was probably a storage room for the previous owner. Warren doesn't go in for ostentatious. Metal desk. One filing cabinet with a framed picture of his brother in full uniform. A pinup calendar, the kind you'd find in an auto repair shop, hangs on an otherwise bare wall. The wait staff jokes about his calendar. Doesn't seem funny to me now.

"I didn't know," I say.

"No one did." He sips from the bottle and sets it down. "So, you can see why I have a problem with you giving away drinks. The liquor's not even mine. It belongs to the IRS."

I point at the bottle. "They gonna miss that?"

"Fuck them."

"No. Fuck you if you think I stole from you. You *know* better."

He sighs. "Yeah, I guess I do. But you'll find work somewhere else. Meanwhile, the Feds are going to take this place over and sell it for parts."

His chest heaves. I worry he's going to cry. "I feel like . . . this is stupid, but . . .I feel like I let my brother down. Wesley. This place is his, too, in a way, and I . . ." He shakes his head and closes his eyes.

I let him breathe.

I came into the office ready for war. Now, I want to hug the little bald bastard. "Is there anything you can do? Have you tried to get a loan?"

"From a bank?" Warren utters a snort, half-laugh and half-sob. "The bank *owns* this place. Now, they get the title, and they get to keep the money I've paid them."

"When do you close the doors?"

He shakes his head again, slower this time, as if he's winding down. "I was going to try for one more weekend, but what's the point? I think we're done now." He pointed at a pile of cash on the desk. "We had a good night. Go out on top, right?"

"Don't deposit the cash," I advise him. "Keep it. The IRS won't miss it, and neither will the bank."

He sighs. "You're probably right."

"I know I'm right. Do you have anything saved?"

His head shake is almost imperceptible now. "Nope. Used it up trying to keep this place floating."

I stand. "You have my address on my W-4. I'm easy to find. If there's ever anything I can do for you, or you need a place to crash, let me know."

His chest heaves again.

"I have a dog, though," I add. "If you're allergic, you'll be out of luck."

Half a smile.

As I turn to leave, he says, "Those guys were your friends?"

"Yes. One's a bartender. The other's a cook."

Warren nods. "I hope I didn't insult them."

"They work in the industry. They're used to taking shit from managers and owners."

This time, he laughs out loud. It's a mournful sound.

Chapter Fifteen
Press Conference

"Journalists are like dogs; whenever anything moves, they begin to bark."
~Arthur Schopenhauer

I drive Sasha up to the mountains on Sunday. The weather may change soon—after all, it's Colorado. I let my pup romp at the river's edge, splashing and jumping like a child playing in a sprinkler. I'm carrying a pocket full of jerky, two beers and a bag of Fritos, planning to make a day of it. The sky is overcast, painted in shades of gray that spill into the water and the rocks. The only other color comes from the pines, like green combs in an old woman's hair.

Poetic, right? I'm the poet laureate of unemployed bartenders.

I plant myself on a flat rock about six feet from the water. In a month, maybe less, the ground will be covered in snow. Ice will rim the banks, though the frigid waters will continue to flow. The splash and burble of the river usually soothes me, but not today. I open a beer and take a sip, then tear open my bag of chips. Sasha realizes food is being consumed and comes running for her first piece of jerky.

I dig the heel of my shoe into the soft ground as I drink, making a hole in the dirt and pebbles. I love the mountains. Just thirty minutes from here, the crazy world is bubbling over like a tiny pot on a high flame. Here? You can be alone. If you know your way, and I do, you can hide where only tracking dogs can find you.

I was born for these mountains. I was not meant to live in glass and aluminum. Years ago, I planned to save my money and buy a cabin in a place like this. Like an alchemist, I would turn the hours spent pouring liquor and cleaning floor mats into a mountain home. A sanctuary of logs. Then, I'd devote the rest of my life to reading and listening to the river.

Perhaps I'd write poetry.

The future doesn't look like that, now. I don't think I'll ever live here. Visiting with Sasha will have to be enough.

Mouth full of jerky, Sasha runs back to the bank as if she's going to jump in, only to wheel around and fling herself back to me. A breeze slips along the cool water and tousles my hair. I wish I'd brought a jacket instead of the second beer.

What will I do next? Bartending jobs are hard to come by. I could ask Billotte to get me on at his place. Humiliating, since I've turned him down whenever he's asked to be my assistant. The irony makes my stomach flip.

My part-time bar job leaves me ineligible for unemployment. Even if I get another part-time gig to tide me over, what's my long-term look like? A real job, I suppose. Certainly not selling hot dogs and lottery tickets at a convenience store.

I know the answer, of course. I've priced the courses necessary to be certified as an investigator. I've shopped online for the computer I'd need. As for my poor car Betsy, I don't think she'd last two weeks working for an investigative firm. I will probably have to buy a new used car. The thought gives my insides another flip. I love that stupid car.

Halfway into beer one, I'm done drinking. I find a piece of driftwood and play fetch with Sasha until she gets tired and wanders off to hide the stick among the rocks. When she returns, I ask, "What now?" She tilts her head, as if to point out that I've asked the only pertinent question—one I'll have to answer for myself.

Driving home, Betsy overheats. I pull over and let the engine cool down. Sasha's hungry again, so I pull into the first available gas station for a second bag of jerky, a gallon of antifreeze, and some radiator sealant. I grab a quart of oil while I'm at it. Only the best for my girls.

* * * * *

Monday morning, I hop downstairs to the bakery. Their front window has been repaired—again—and they are open for business. Adella, the tiny woman who usually takes my order, greets me with a big smile. "We have muffins with gluten in them today," she says. This is a surprise. Such delicacies are normally gone by the time I crawl out of bed. I order two muffins, a carton of apple juice, and a newspaper.

Just outside the bakery, there are two tables with chairs. The morning is cold, but sitting outdoors still seems like a fine idea. The front page of the paper contains the national news. A new treaty with China. Terrorist attacks in Europe. A funeral for a judge who recently passed.

I open to page two to see the local news, and learn that Downtown Chicken has closed, at least temporarily. A surprising number of facts are absent from the article. Who closed the doors, the restaurant or the city? What was the reason for the closure? The article mentions an ongoing conflict with Health and Environment but doesn't say if the conflict led to the closing. And when did they shut down? It's Monday morning, and here's the article spread out in front of me, catching crumbs from my muffin. When I spoke to Lloyd on Saturday, they were still open. The private investigator in me decides the restaurant must have closed sometime between Saturday night and this morning.

A sidebar article lists previous businesses at that location. A bakery. A Mexican cafeteria. A coffee shop. A Mediterranean grill. The implication was clear—the corner spells doom for restaurants.

The local page does not mention Wesley's. Warren's place was open for business twice as long as Mo's. It's not fair that his grill would disappear without someone taking notice.

I find a note at the bottom of the page. Armando de San Martín will be at the municipal building today to officially pitch a new community center project.

Page three covers sports. My teams lost.

I skip the ads. Shoving the last of the muffin in my mouth, I head home. The second muffin is for Sasha. She has a sweet tooth. And she likes gluten.

Inside, I check my Cave of the Winds clock. I have time to walk my pup, wash up, and head for the municipal building. The councilman's announcement might prove to be interesting.

* * * * *

Councilman Armando de San Martín stands outside of the City Planner's office. The wide hallway inside the municipal building features vaulted ceilings, skylights, and shiny tile floors. A half-dozen reporters are in attendance, one of whom must certainly represent our local paper. The others? A mystery. The local television station has a camera set up, and at least one radio station is doing a feed. I may have misunderstood what is happening here. I had expected a photo op. This seems more like a press conference.

The councilman wears the expensive jacket I saw hanging in his office. Looks better on him than on a hook. He has an odd way of standing, shoulders erect, head held high, yet informal. Casually imperial. I can stand in front of a mirror for hours and not pull that off.

"In the past," he says, "a sense of community helped people to know they mattered. That they weren't alone. That their needs would be met by a shared commitment. Over time, the pact eroded, and along with it, the safety net that provided comfort even in the darkest of times. Our community center has played an important role in restoring our faith in that time-honored notion—a faith more important now than at any other time in our recent history. Unfortunately, our unprecedented need has outgrown the current facility.

"We propose moving the community center into the downtown area. Let the proximity to this building, the seat of our local government, provide the kind of synergy necessary to reinvigorate both our city officials and our community spirit."

He pauses, shifting his stance. "I was speaking to someone recently, who noted, quite correctly, that a community center ought to be near the center of the community." Soft laughter. "I wholeheartedly agree. These are challenging times. The unfortunate difficulties of downtown businesses may provide a silver lining—an opportunity benefitting both the business community and the community at large. This much is certain—a vibrant community center will draw business to Old Town Westbrook again.

"Today, I presented the City Planner with a proposal for a downtown community center. The proposal would nearly triple the present facility's floor space. Westbrook could not normally afford this plan, though one could argue the city can't afford *not* to build a downtown center. I am asking the members of our community to come together behind our proposal. Your direct input will go a long way toward engendering support for this most worthy of causes."

He smiled, and spread his arms, palms up. "Now, I am prepared to answer your questions." The sole female reporter in the group raises her arm, and the councilman nods in her direction. "Shelly?"

"Given the demographics of those who used the old facility, does the failure to provide adequate space demonstrate a reluctance on the city's part to address minority concerns?"

Armando de San Martín sighs and looks down. The momentarily slumped shoulders and tired expression are a convincing show of regret. "A fair question, but not one on which I'd choose to focus. It is true that the center is home to a number of advocacy groups and community outreach programs. And it is also true that people of color constitute the larger portion of active participants at the current location. But our city has always supported forward-thinking programs, which is why I'm excited about the prospects for a new center."

The reporter who asked the question nods and makes a note in her pad. Everyone else is recording videos on their cellphones.

Another reporter asks how much space the new facility will require.

The councilman grins. "I hate to sound greedy, but. . . all of it." The reporters laugh appreciatively.

This isn't a press conference. This is a ballet.

I scan the dancers, and am surprised to find Naomi Adriana, Walter's second-in-command, leaning against a wall. Her face is drawn in and puckered. Is she here because she's working behind the scenes with the councilman? Or is she here because she wants to make sure her department isn't thrown under the bus?

To the councilman's left, two men stand, arms folded. I've seen one of them lifting weights at the community center—a big man with a serious expression. I also recalled seeing him across the center's lobby, chatting with the councilman. Was he an employee?

"Do you have cost estimates for your proposal?"

"No. My proposal is still in the theoretical phase. Frankly, we were spurred to action by the business community's news over the weekend, encouraged that we had a solution for the concerns of all the stakeholders in the current situation."

I've seen blueprints. The man just lied.

I wait for a follow-up question. The timing between the "temporary" closure of Downtown Chicken and the proposal for the new center seems obvious. Isn't anyone going to ask about the timing?

One of the reporters, a chubby man with a swayed back, asks, "We've heard a rumor that you and your family are planning a vacation?"

"*Jesus,*" I whisper.

The councilman's smile is beatific. "I can confirm that rumor. My daughter recently graduated with a political science degree from UCLA, and she's marrying her long-time boyfriend. My wife and I are flying out for the wedding, then on to Hawaii for some rest and relaxation."

"Congratulations," one of the reporters said. "Is your daughter a chip off the old block?"

Armando de San Martín shakes his head. "She's a fireball. She's going to do greater things than I could ever have dreamed."

"How is it you already have blueprints ready for the new community center?"

The reporters freeze. Armando de San Martín's face is a blank. The crowd looks around to see who's asked the question. I am mildly surprised to find I'm the culprit.

"That's not correct," the Councilman says. "We hope to begin the design process as soon as the city indicates—"

"I saw the blueprints," I say, but the murmur of dissent from those around me blankets my words.

"Where's your press pass?" the man next to me demands.

"Troll," growls another. I have stepped into the group of reporters, and they glare at me. I am not one of them. I am not in the club. The television camera man lowers his camera. To my right, a security guard approaches, a grim look on his face.

"As I said, the project is in its initial phase. You've been misinformed." He gave a slight bow. "Ladies and gentlemen, I thank you for your time." The Councilman slides to his left, flanked by the two men I'd noticed earlier. I try to push my way closer, but the security guard is in front of me before I can blink. He's a pro.

"Councilman?" I call.

Armando de San Martín stops, a frown on his face. Shielded by the guard, he steps closer and says, "You're the boxer, aren't you?" The men flanking him mirror his moves. Bodyguards.

"I am, sir."

He leans even closer, his voice low. "I understand you used the men's room as a boxing ring last week."

I glance around, surprised that the councilman would be so candid in the presence of reporters, but they're backing away, snapping pictures of me instead. "That's true," I say. "When they cleaned up Santi's blood, did they find his knife?"

The reporters are silent and sullen. Where is their curiosity? There's more going on here than meets the eye, and they don't seem to care.

"I don't know what your agenda is," the Councilman says. "But I don't condone violence and I never have. Whatever your cause, you do it an injustice." He turns and leaves, still flanked by his two men. The large one, the weightlifter, glances back as if memorizing my face.

"Come with me," the security guard says. "I have a few questions for you."

He grabs my arm and pulls. I let him.

The security guard will ask my name and address, and I'll give it to him. He will pretend he can have me prosecuted. This is a city facility, and I have transgressed. I will appear contrite. He will be joined by other guards, who will stare, grim-faced. They will eventually let me go, probably with a threat. I will be duly chastened.

No matter. I have another piece to the puzzle. This whole mess is being orchestrated. Armando de San Martín and Walter Mason may be working together to steal Mo Brown's restaurant.

Things aren't always what they seem. The councilman, who looks like a straight arrow, is flying crooked. Mo Brown, who looks like a thug, may be a victim. Naomi Adriana may well be involved, too, perhaps as Walter's go-between. Or maybe Walter isn't moving fast enough, and she's the councilman's whip hand. Either way, I find myself wondering if I've accidentally identified the right party in the matter of Walter Mason's blackmailing.

Chapter Sixteen
Lights Out

"What opera isn't violent? Two things happen, violence and love. And other than that, name something else. You can't."
~Cab Calloway

Tuesday's paper carries an article on the Councilman's press conference with a vague description of the proposed project, emphasizing the exchange about the city and race relations, along with a passing mention of the closure of Downtown Chicken. I'm shocked I'm not mentioned. I'll have to wait for my fifteen minutes of fame.

I spend Monday night following Zoey. Once again, she does not go home. I have a vague suspicion she'll show up in the company of one or more of the players in this game. Perhaps drinks with the Councilman, or coffee with Naomi. Instead, she leads me on another shopping expedition. As before, she focuses on value, avoiding the boutique stores. I wonder why she doesn't shop online. Perhaps getting away from her husband is the point of the exercise.

I promised Kelly Mason I'd keep an open mind. That means giving equal time to the idea that Walter *isn't* spearheading this mess. But he's involved. What I don't know is his exact role in this nasty little affair.

Finding out might be easier without certain constraints. I could get a sense of things if I could talk to Walter himself, but I'm not supposed to do that. On the other hand, if Walter's knee-deep in the conspiracy, then he won't open up to me. I am, after all, the guy who blew the whistle on his affair. Which makes me wonder how that revelation played out in the Mason household. Zoey seems to be unaware of any drama. Perhaps Walter hasn't told her. Or perhaps Kelly is holding onto the information like an ace in the hole in whatever card game she's playing.

Either way, I'm more likely to get useful information from Mo Brown. I am reluctant to meet him face-to-face since he'll likely try to punch mine. However, I think I'm going to have to pay him a visit.

I take a walk over to Downtown Chicken. I don't know for certain he's hanging around a closed restaurant in the middle of the day. I'm just guessing. I would be if it was *my* business. I'd be like Warren, hiding in a back room at Wesley's, unable to let go. Bottle of something distilled next to a smudged glass.

The front doors are locked. A notice of closure from the Health and Environment Department hangs on the inside of the glass. The lights are out, and I can't see anyone moving around.

I decide to try the upstairs offices. There's an entrance to the stairway on the Main Street side, but it's locked, too. I circle the alley behind the restaurant and climb a metal stairway to the second floor. That door is open, and I go inside.

There are three upstairs offices. The largest is reserved for the owner's group. I peer in through the glass door. Nobody home. I check the other two offices. One is empty. The second is a telecom sales operation in full swing. I poke my head in the door, and a chirpy woman with big hair asks if I'm applying for a job. I tell her I'm in the wrong place—the most heartfelt thing I've said in days—and head back into the hall.

Two more doors. One is a unisex restroom. The other opens to a stairway. I creep down as if I'm about to get pinched for B&E. At the bottom, I find the back entrance to Downtown Chicken, unlocked. I take a deep breath and step inside.

Mo's office is just beyond the door. He's sitting at his computer, a pair of reading glasses perched on his flat nose. He looks up at me, a blank look on his face. Perhaps he's beyond surprise.

"Hello, Mo," I say. Remembering the telecom office upstairs, I say the first thing that comes to mind. "I'm here about the job."

A grin flashes across his face. It's only there for an instant, but the scowl that replaces it can't wipe away the memory. "Funny. What the fuck are you doing here?"

I consider extending a hand, but he might snap it off rather than shake it. My smart-ass mouth only bought me a second's grace, so I talk fast. "My name is Slag Ferguson. I'm a private investigator." Now, that's something I've never said before. I guess I've decided to make it true. I'll have to sign up for courses and buy a Fedora.

I continue. "I've been hired to look into some threats made against my client." He's shifting in his chair, so I put my lips in high gear. "Whatever's going on seems to involve the city's attempt to steal your restaurant from you."

There. I've thrown my best pitch—the only pitch that might work. He'll either listen, or he'll bash my head in.

"I'm listening." His eyelids are at half-mast, and he's poised to spring, but I'm still breathing, so that's good.

"It's pretty clear to me your troubles with Health and Environment have to do with shutting you down and turning this place into a community center. I've seen the blueprints. They've been planning this for a while."

Mo tilts his head, and his legs—giant pistons planted for action—seem to relax. "*Motherfucker*. I *told* him the Councilman was involved." He shakes his big head. "Go on."

I lean against the office doorframe, trying to appear relaxed. Meanwhile, my heart is skipping rope. "My client—"

"Who is your client?"

"I can't tell you that, Mo. But I can tell you somebody is blackmailing someone. I came here to look you in the eye and ask if it's you."

This is bad form on my part. But I'm not trying to get information. I'm trying to measure Mo Brown. Sometimes, you have to go with your gut.

"I don't know what the *fuck* you're talking about. What does this have to do with my restaurant?" His legs are tensing again. I swear I can see his calves swell.

"It's possible you're blackmailing city officials to keep your restaurant open."

Mo sits back, his hands on his knees. His expression shifts again. Half smile, half snarl, narrowed gaze. "If that's so, it ain't working. My place is *closed*, isn't it?"

"Right." I'm thinking on my feet now, so I guess my fear factor has diminished. I have an important question to ask, and I want an honest answer. I know people lie. But we're here alone, no audience, and there's no reason for him not to answer me. "I understand you only own part of this place."

Mo's gaze narrows even more. He's watching me through eye slits again.

"The boys upstairs are the majority owners?"

"I own five percent," he says.

I don't breathe. I know the truth when I hear it.

"What else?" he asks.

"So, you're the front man?"

He nods.

"You put any money of your own into this?"

He nods his big head. "What I had. Friends back East put me with the investors."

"And investors just opened their wallets for you?"

Mo flashes a thin smile. "I have important friends."

"Okay. But it's just five percent. Why are you fighting so hard to stay open?"

His shoulders and chest heave, as if he's coughed, or laughed once. Or maybe he's fighting tears of rage. He shakes his head. "My recipes. My staff. My sweat and tears. Do you have any idea what that means? It's mine. *This place is mine.*"

"Five percent."

"It's *my* five percent. Those motherfuckers upstairs can worry about their ninety-five. I'm defending what's *mine*. I didn't steal this shit. I *built* it. They don't have the balls to come at me with a gun or a knife. They come at me with *regulations*. Was a time in my life when I'd have ended some motherfuckers over this shit. But I'm a *businessman* now. This is my *business*. And they're *not* taking this away from me."

"I assume you have a lawyer."

"Oh, the boys upstairs hired lawyers. Little white boys with big invoices." He sits back, snarling. His teeth are showing. "As for your blackmail shit, I don't know what the *fuck* you are talking about. You need to back your ass on outa here, because *I'm* the *black male* you need to worry about right now."

True. "Thanks for your time," I say. "I hope things break your way." I mean it. I leave the way I came in.

As I climb the stairs on my way back to the alley, I think hard. I don't know for certain that Mo Brown isn't blackmailing Walter Mason. I'm guessing not. I do know that what's happening here is wrong. And whoever's calling Walter, threatening him with Zoey, this little piece of real estate is involved.

* * * * *

At the end of the day, I head to Billotte's bar for a few beers and a dose of the kind of crazy I know and understand. He's supposed to introduce me to a girl—someone from the bar he's tending—but she doesn't show. He doesn't seem concerned. "We spent the night," he says. "Easy *cum*, easy go."

I don't laugh.

"Do you see what I did there?" he asks.

"You realize you have a problem with women, don't you?"

Suddenly, Billotte is serious. Smile gone. Voice lowered, with a touch of the dramatic. "I'm not the one with a problem."

Irritated, I wait for him to elaborate.

Billotte takes his time, sipping at a shot of whiskey, which is clearly for my benefit. This may be the first time in his life he's sipped anything. Just as I think about punching him, he starts talking. "I haven't seen you with anyone since your wife did you wrong. Why is that?"

Serious questions deserve a serious answer. "I had enough punishment," is what comes out.

"You don't have to answer this, but did she ever love you?"

That throws me for a moment. It's a question I've asked and answered for myself, but admitting it out loud? Then again, this is Billotte. "I don't think so. She liked the attention I gave her. She liked being taken care of. But she wanted more. Obviously. And she didn't think much of my job. There's no money in restaurant work."

"No shit," Billotte says. He finishes his shot and waves at the bartender for another round. Still looking away, he asks, "You gonna start dating? Or are you all through with love?"

"Love?" I snort.

Billotte turns just a bit, looking at me now out of the corner of his eye. "Don't think it exists?"

"Don't tell me about the wonders of love. Where's *your* girl tonight?"

"She's probably home, sore," Billotte says. "And don't change the subject."

The bartender delivers Billotte's shot and my beer. I take a sip and ask, "What was the subject?"

"I'll recap for you. Love doesn't exist because women are treacherous bitches."

"Love exists. I loved my ex. That was real enough." I mean this to sound ironic, but it comes out pathetic. I down my drink.

"Okay, I take it back. Women are treacherous bitches, and only *you* know what love is, because you're so special."

I don't say anything. Billotte is in a mood, and he's pushing every button I have. He's about to get stuck with the tab.

He puts a hand on my shoulder. "You're kind of a narcissist, Slag."

I knock his hand away. "Let's establish your credentials," I say. "Have you had a relationship that lasted longer than three months in the entire time I've known you?"

The crazy look, the one that precedes a punch, isn't there. His eyes are dark and serious. "I believe in love. Just not for me. I'm not relationship material. I know that, and I don't hang around long enough to ruin anybody's life." He licks his lips. "But you? You're still looking for the perfect woman. Half-hooker, half-angel. She doesn't exist, and that includes

Kelly Mason." My face must give me away because he waves a finger at me. "You have the hots for her. Don't even try to deny it. But she sweats and poops, same as all of them."

"I think of my clients as clients."

"Are you telling me you wouldn't jump her bones if you had the chance?"

Of course, I would.

"Well?" he demands.

"My wife cheats on me, and it ruins my life, so I'm going to turn around and ruin someone else's life by cheating with a married woman? That's not logical."

Billotte shrugs, unperturbed. "The heart is a moron."

I can't disagree. But I find myself wanting to argue anyway.

The bar is nearly deserted. The old-school video games, vintage concert posters, and seventies wall art decorating the establishment seem outdated and forlorn—something I can relate to. I wonder if this place will last. The bartender, a skinny kid with a stained white shirt, is watching college basketball on the television over the bar. He's not going home with a full wallet tonight. Billotte ordered wings—a throwback to the Tap and Wing—but they're not good. Each wing is tiny, and there's too much butter in the sauce. The celery sticks were cut days ago and stored in water, judging by the soggy brown ends.

"You haven't jumped her bones so far, have you? You didn't make that mistake, right?" His voice is low.

Mine is not. "I treat my clients like clients."

"Hookers have clients."

"God damn it, Billotte, you're being a pain in the ass tonight."

Billotte shrugs again. "You hate it when I'm right."

"You guys okay?" The bartender keeps his distance, a worried look on his face. Have we been getting too loud?

"We're good," I say, reaching for my wallet. "I'll tab out."

Billotte looks at his watch. "It's nine o'clock. Are you going home to cry?"

I put the wallet back in my pocket. "You can pay the tab." I grab my jacket off the bar stool and leave before he can argue.

Enough is enough. My life is pissing me off right now, and I need to go home.

The bar is situated on the east side of Old Town Plaza. I don't want to see or talk to anyone, so I wind my way through the alleys, behind the bars and brewhouses, past dumpsters and broken furniture, my hands jammed in my pockets. Clouds overhead. No moon or stars. It isn't raining, but there's mist in the air dampening the sound of my footsteps. A solitary floodlight at the back of one building pales to a feeble yellow color. I think of a line from a T.S. Eliot poem—"Not with a bang, but with a whimper." Good old T.S.—a regular Nostra-dumbass.

Up ahead, three silhouettes block the alley. I'm passing an adjoining alley, so I turn left. I'm not interested in seeing anyone. I don't want to nod a hello as I pass by. I want to be alone. But when I near the end of the alley, the same three men step into view. I may be in trouble.

I stop. They stand twenty feet away. Too dark to see their faces. I recall another phrase, attributed to the Brit, Admiral Nelson. "Never mind the maneuvers. Go straight at them." And I do.

This seems to surprise them, and one backs up a step. Closing in, I see that they are Latino. I wipe my eyes. It's starting to rain.

I veer to the right, moving through the tiny gap vacated by the one who backed away, but they close ranks, fists cocked. I square up without thinking, ready to fight.

We stand there, not moving. "Well?" I ask, but there's no answer. I hear the rain and something else. Too late, I recognize the sound as footsteps. Behind me. That's when I go to sleep.

Chapter Seventeen
Head Games

"There is laughter because there is nothing to laugh at."
~Theodor W. Adorno

In the movies, the hero has a sixth sense about an attack coming from behind. At the last moment, he turns, or tilts his head just enough to avoid the blow. Then, outraged at the cowardice of a back attack, he dispenses justice in swift, brutal fashion.

In real life, the tire iron hits, and though it's a glancing blow, it sounds like a baseball bat hitting a watermelon. In real life, the victim is out when his face bounces on the pavement, leaving a strawberry on his left cheek. Later, when he wakes up in the hospital, bruised and stupid, the first question he hears throws him for a loop.

"How are you feeling?" A woman dressed in scrubs stands at the foot of my bed. I'm in an emergency room bay—curtained on three sides. The machine to my right beeps like an unbuckled seat belt. I try to focus my eyes, which is not easy with the overhead light. The woman wears a nametag.

"I can't read your nametag," I say.

"You've had a concussion," she says. "There's a nasty lump on the back of your head, and some swelling and abrasions on your cheek."

I nod, then wince. My head feels like Sugar Ray's speed bag. Leonard or Robinson. All them Sugars could punch.

The nurse has her eyes on her watch and her fingers on my wrist. Though her hands are scrubbed clean, they are soft, not dry. I like the sensation. After a moment, she lets go. "What happened to you?"

A wave of nausea rolls through me. I close my eyes. I don't want to vomit in front of this woman. I hold still and focus on settling my stomach.

"Are you with me?" she asks.

"Literally or metaphorically?" I ask. It's a clever thing to say. My mind may be muddy, but my mouth is its usual charming self.

She gives me half a smile. "I need to ask you a few questions. And I need literal answers."

"Shoot."

"Have you suffered any previous head injuries?"

Aside from years of boxing? "Never."

I have to be careful. The truth can get me a room overnight and a bill I can't pay. Nevertheless, I answer the rest of her questions honestly. No, I don't have blood clotting issues. I'm not taking any medication other than beer and liquor. When she places an ice bag on the right side of my head, I wince, but I don't scream or tell her to be careful. "I still can't read your name tag."

"Corrin," she says. "I'll be here until midnight. When the new shift comes on—"

"I'll be gone," I finish.

"We're going to keep you overnight—"

"I'm not sure who you mean by *we*, but unless *we* includes paying the tab, you are mistaken."

Corrin is a brunette with eyes the color of sea foam—a soft green. She's not wearing a lot of makeup. I like that. Heavy makeup is like spray painting a blue jay. Natural is good. I think she's in her twenties, but I can't be sure. I glance at her ring hand. Nothing there. When I look back, her head is tilted as if she's reading my mind. "How's the pain?" she asks.

"I've had worse."

"When you go home—*tomorrow*—stay away from aspirin or ibuprofen. They can cause bleeding. Take acetaminophen instead." She pauses. "The hospital can set you up with a payment plan, you know."

"No job," I say. "No paycheck, no payments." I start to sit up and swing one leg over the edge of the bed.

"You really should wait until the doctor comes by."

"I guess so. My head is swimming like Mark Spitz."

"I'm sorry. I don't know who that is."

I sigh. "He was an Olympic swimming champion. My jokes are wasted on the young."

"You aren't that old." She pauses. "You are funny, though." She has a sly kind of smile, and she's turning it on me. I forget I'm in pain for a moment.

Only a moment.

I sit up and manage not to vomit. My mouth tastes like Blood and Sand. Not the classic scotch cocktail from a hundred years ago. Sand, like on a beach. Blood, like what's all over the back of my hand. "May I have some water?" I ask.

"All you want," she says. "No more beer for a while, though." She must be able to smell it on me. Not a happy realization. "How much did you have to drink?" she asks. Maybe she can read minds.

"Three beers," I say.

"That's a fair amount."

"No. That's lunch." I take a small cup of water from her. It tastes sweet. "I think I'm feeling okay," I say. "Almost normal." I tap the IV taped to the back of my hand. "Could you unhook me, please?"

"I really think you should wait until the doctor sees you," she repeats. Her voice is a shade lower now. I like a woman with a husky voice. "The results from your panels should be back soon."

"Panels?"

"The blood tests they took when they put in the IV."

"Yeah, they didn't need to do that. I got whacked on the head. My blood is just fine."

"Normal procedure," she explains. "The man who brought you in said you were hit with a tire iron. You're lucky to be alive."

"Is he still here?"

"Robert? I think so. Charming man, your friend."

I search her face and find hints of sarcasm. She's at the computer now, typing something. She's either chatty, or she's trying to distract me. "So, why did they jump you? Were you robbed?"

I pat my wallet, grateful to be wearing my pants instead of one of those hospital gowns opening up at the ass. "No, not robbed. Maybe Billotte chased them off before they could finish."

"Billotte? Robert?"

"Italian name." I manage a smile. "Corrin is an unusual name, too." She doesn't respond. "I get to ask you questions too, right?"

"I didn't hear a question." Her lips aren't smiling, but her eyes are. Beautiful eyes. Cute, pixie face. The uniform tries to hide her figure and fails. Her hair is pinned, and I wonder what it looks like down around her shoulders.

"You're going to need to rest for a while. No television. No computers."

"Don't own either one."

"Long naps."

"I don't sleep."

"You are a *difficult* patient," she says, smiling. She walks to the bay curtain, ready to slip outside.

"Can I speak to Bobby? Robert?"

She looks back over her shoulder. "I'll bring him back in a few minutes. Don't go anywhere, hear me?"

As soon as she's gone, I stand, hand to the bed for balance. When I can move, I pull the IV needle free. There's a little blood, so I take gauze from the table and press it to the back of my hand. Then, I sit on the side of the bed and wait. Just when I start to wonder if she's forgotten me, she leads Billotte into the room.

"You're unhooked," she says.

"Sorry. I gotta go."

"Please wait."

I agree, if only to make her happy.

She promises to find the physician on duty. I think she's afraid I'll duck out. Once she's gone, I turn to Bobby. "What happened? I can't remember shit."

He sits down on the visitor's chair, a worried look on his face. "When you got pissed off and left the bar, I went after you. You were halfway up an alley, and all of a sudden, you turned left. There was a guy on the corner, and you walked right past him, so, no big deal, right? Except, as soon as you walk by, he follows you, and he's got something in his hand."

"I didn't see anybody."

"That's obvious."

"It was dark. It was raining."

"Are you going to let me tell the story?" he asks.

I nod. Gently, so my head doesn't detach.

"Okay," he continues. "So I hustle up to the turn, and there you are, facing three guys with a fourth one creeping up behind you. I see he's got a tire iron, and before I can yell anything, he whacks you in your melon. You go down like a prom date."

"Nice metaphor. What happened next?"

"He didn't get all of you. It looked like he was going to take another swing, so I yelled at them and they took off."

"You're lucky they didn't come after you."

"I'd have run like hell. Anyway, I was pretty sure you were dead, but then you sat up and started yelling at me, telling me not to call an ambulance."

"I don't remember that," I said. "Doesn't surprise me, though. You know how much those damned things cost?"

"No," Billotte says. "Probably a lot. But you have savings, don't you?"

"They're draining away as we speak."

We're silent for a moment. Billotte stares at me and asks, "Do you know who they were?"

I think before I answer. "I didn't recognize anyone. I only saw the one guy's face, and he didn't look familiar." I shake my head just a little. It hurts. "I had a few words with Armando de San Martín at his press conference yesterday. He has security guards, and he might hold a grudge."

"Minnie's ex has a problem with you, too."

"Yeah. I have fans all over town."

Billotte slumps back in the plastic visitor's chair, steepling his fingers over his chest. "I thought you were dead."

"Don't make a big deal about it." That sounds ungrateful, even to me, so I add, "Thanks for getting me here. Wanna split the tab?"

"I paid before I left the bar."

"I mean the hospital tab."

"Fuck you," he says, grinning.

The doctor arrives, Corrin at his heels. "You're supposed to be in bed," he says.

"I'm headed out. I was just waiting for you."

"You need to be here overnight. You suffered a serious head injury."

"Mr. Ferguson is hard-headed," Corrin adds helpfully. Billotte laughs. Even he gets the double meaning.

The doctor is a slender man with slumped shoulders and a gray beard, neatly trimmed. "If the blow had landed a half-inch closer to your ear, we wouldn't be conversing. That's how close you came to death, young man."

"You almost bought the farm," Billotte says, acting as interpreter.

"Can't buy anything. I'm unemployed."

Corrin's half-smile is back, which pleases me.

The doctor's frown deepens, and he huffs a little. "If you go home AMA, you run the risk of seizure, infection, internal bleeding—"

"What's AMA?" I ask.

"Against medical advice," Corrin explains.

The doctor's frown deepens. "With head trauma, observation for the first twenty-four hours is critical. If you have internal bleeding, for example, you wouldn't necessarily know until it was too late."

"I'll roll the dice," I say. He recoils as if insulted. "It's a tradeoff, Doctor. I appreciate the risks. But I have to balance the risks against the very real problem of paying the tab."

The doctor, irritated, dismisses my concerns with a wave. "In the end, that's your decision. It depends on whether you value your own health." He tells Corrin to note something on my chart, using acronyms, which is probably for the best. I don't want to know.

The doctor turns to leave. I call out a "thank you," but he shows no sign I was heard. I laugh. "I think I made him mad."

"You have a problem with authority," Billotte says. He's pandering, and Corrin rewards him with a nod of agreement. I frown at him.

"Are you sure you won't reconsider leaving?" she asks me.

"AMA," I say. "That stands for *already moving away.*"

"Well," Corrin says, "you have a good sense of humor, Mr. Ferguson."

"Call me Slag," I tell her.

* * * * *

I spend the next thirty minutes wedged in a chair, trying to stay upright in the billing department. The hospital's concern for my welfare has evolved into a concern for my ability to pay the bill, which was *my* concern all along. The mild euphoria of waking up alive and meeting Corrin is gone. In its place is a throbbing, metallic ache making my vision shimmer.

"Payment is due when services are rendered," says the elderly woman behind the desk. She notes my lack of insurance, photocopies my I.D., verifies my home address, cellphone number and other means of identification. "Can you pay this bill with a credit card?" Her voice is a needle. If blood runs from my ears, I won't be surprised.

"When you say, *a* credit card, do you mean someone else's card? Because I don't have a credit card. Are you volunteering *your* card?"

I take her scowl as a no. "Debit card?"

"I have a debit card, but there's no money in my account."

"No insurance and no credit card?" Her brow creases, and her lips twist at the corners. She's old enough to be someone's grandmother. She should be at home, wearing an apron and baking banana bread, not shaking down concussion victims.

We eventually settle on a signature verification of my responsibility for payment, though I stop short of signing a payment agreement. "I'm aware you want me to sign, ma'am, but I am unemployed. If I said I was going to pay you on a regular basis, I'd be lying."

I have money, of course, but it's earmarked for a computer and some courses so I can be certified as a genuine private investigator. Sometime soon, I'll need to get a new apartment. Damage deposit, first month, maybe last month's rent? And Betsy needs more work done than a forty-year-old stripper. I'll pay the damned bill, but not until I'm ready.

Maybe Billotte should have left me in the alley. At least I'd have died with enough cash to bury me.

Slumped in my chair and cradling my head, I say, "I have to go. I can come back again for more punishment in a day or two, but not right now. Someone hit me with a tire iron tonight."

"Oh, that's not good," she says. Her tone is flat and disapproving, as if being attacked was my choice. I get up to leave. She's still talking, but I can't hear her. My ears ring with the music of a crushing headache. I do a little stutter-step leaving the office, and Billotte is there to grab my arm.

"I've got you," he says.

"Thanks," I say, adding, "Just get me out of here."

"Are you sure you should be leaving?"

No, I'm not sure at all. I lied to Corrin about not passing out, and I'm a little foggy on the details of the evening. But they'd have done a CT scan and kept me overnight, and that alone would have eaten up the last of my money.

"You seemed like you when you were flirting with the nurse," Billotte says, "but now, you look like shit. Want me to take you back to the ER?"

"Nope. Gotta feed Sasha."

By the time we reach the end of the hall, Billotte begins to scold me. "What the hell, Slag? You trying to fight the whole world at once?"

"Three against one isn't bad."

"Four. Four against one. I don't care how good a boxer you were. What the hell was going through your mind?"

"A tire iron."

Billotte tries not to laugh, but he can't help himself.

Chapter Eighteen
Flipping the Clock

"Character, like a photograph, develops in darkness."
~Yousuf Karsh

Billotte doesn't own a car, but he's arranged a driver via phone app. In front of the hospital, we climb into a two-tone Ford Fiesta. Green and rust. Half the back seat is stacked with boxes, so Billotte sits in back and I sit up front. The driver is a rumpled little fellow with a chin curtain and a bald head. He introduces himself. "Hi. I'm Bob."

"I'm Bob, too!" Billotte says from behind me.

For the next ten minutes, the two Bobs exchange wisdom about all things Bob. Mothers call their boys "Robert" when they're angry. Bob Ross was the greatest painter in history. Bob spelled backwards is Bob. Each new revelation drives a needle deeper into my skull.

The new Bob is a pointlessly aggressive driver. I lurch from side-to-side as the Fiesta whips in and out of traffic, delivering us a full thirty seconds earlier than a sane driver might have managed. Billotte pays the tab. I thank him, which is all I have the energy for. He pats my shoulder and tells me to take care of myself.

Inside the apartment building, I go straight to the bathroom. One glance in the mirror chills me. My cheek is scabbing over, wet and weeping. Black rings circle my eyes. A huge bandage, like a sanitary napkin, is taped to the right side of my head. I look like a corpse on its period. So much for making a good impression with the nurse.

Then, I remember Sasha. I have to walk her.

I expect a puddle by the front door, but my poor girl is holding it in like a champ. I take her out, trying not to move my head as I walk, which is next to impossible with my wrist attached to a leash.

It's raining. I can't smell wildfire smoke, so that's a good thing. In fact, I can't smell anything at all. Perhaps the rain is dousing the fires and washing down the dumpsters.

Sasha does her business. I've forgotten to bring plastic bags, so I end up leaving her poop in the alley. All I want to do is lay down. Perhaps the soft rain will lull me.

But when I finally put my head to a pillow, I can't get comfortable. Sasha tries to settle in, but I thrash my way through the night, so after a while, she jumps down and lies on the floor. She loves me, but not enough to spend the night wrestling.

* * * * *

When I wake again, Sasha is still on the floor, staring at me. I start to move, but immediately think better of it. Every cell in my body screams. My bed sheet is soaked in sweat. I'm going to have to wash it. I lever myself up with my elbows, not quite sitting, and wait for the nausea to subside. I can turn my head—a little—and a glance tells me it's still dark. I hear noise outside the window but identifying it will have to wait. I have one urgent need.

I must get to the bathroom.

Sitting now, I rest in place. Sasha whines. Does she know I'm hurting?

With supreme effort, I stand, one hand on the bedroom bookcase for support. My skull feels as if it's been carved out and filled with hornets. I close my eyes, trying not to sway. I would stand here for a while, but my bladder won't stop shouting.

I stumble into the office, hand along the wall, and stare at my Cave of the Winds clock. Eight. The sun should be up by now. Was there an eclipse

I didn't know about? I cross behind my desk and look out my window. Protesters fill the plaza.

A sudden realization crosses my addled mind. I grab my cellphone. Eight o'clock. My Cave of the Winds memorabilia was right. It's eight o'clock. At night.

I've slept through the day. That's why I need the bathroom and Sasha needs a walk.

Despite the urgency, it takes me a long time to get dressed. In the bathroom, I check my cheek first. It's raw and crusted. My eyes look worse, too, ringed with black and yellow.

Sasha needs attention, but I make a side trip to the community toilet before leashing her. She's impatient, pulling hard as I head for the stairs. I have no sense of balance, and almost pitch down the steps. In the alley, her mess from the previous night waits like an accusation. I've forgotten the poop bags again.

Old Town plaza is filling up. I don't know what new atrocity stirred the protestor's pot. I'll have to check my cellphone when I'm safe in my office.

The throbbing in my head reminds me I need acetaminophen. I don't have any in the apartment. Plenty of ibuprofen, but the nurse—Corrin— said ibuprofen might make my brain bleed.

I return Sasha to the apartment and feed her. My poor girl has an irresponsible dad.

I should have stayed in the hospital.

But if I had, who would have taken care of Sasha?

What if I died? What would become of her? I sit at my desk and consider the possibilities, but pain makes the effort pointless. Without a trip to the convenience store, my head is going to implode. I pull on a jacket and glance at the wall clock. Nine o'clock. I've been awake for an hour.

I tell Sasha, "Be good. I'll be right back." She stares at me as if to ask why a responsible adult doesn't keep basics like acetaminophen on hand. Well, Sasha, I don't have a real bathroom. Hence, there's no bathroom cabinet. I'm in my thirties, and I'm an unemployed bartender without a bathroom.

Outside, festivities are in full swing. The crowd has doubled in size. I still don't know the cause, and now I don't care. Getting dressed took too much out of me. As I walk, the first drops of an impending storm begin to fall.

Petrichor. The word pops into my head like a memory. It means the smell of rain. Only I can't smell *anything.* I think my head is broken.

On my way to the convenience store, I realize just how deep the night is. Heaven's lights are blocked by the clouds, and the earthbound lights of the city turn the streets into a shadowbox. Elongated strips of black crisscross the sidewalk, as if I'm walking through Dr. Caligari's Cabinet.

Feels like I'm tilting to the left. The whole world might slide to the side. If I fall, I'm going to seriously hurt myself. I stop and try to get my bearings, hands on my hips. I close my eyes, but only for a moment. Closing my eyes makes me dizzy.

It's raining fat drops now. The wet streets look like fresh tar. A car passes by, throwing spray in its wake. The violent, drenching rain is all I can hear. If any birds stayed in Westbrook instead of going south, they're drowning in the trees.

I reach the store and step inside, grateful to be out of the rain. Hovering near the front door, trying to remember. Oh, yes. *Acetaminophen.* Anything else? Something to eat? I wish the place had a deli. I'd take home a hot meal.

Home. I'm already tired, and the walk home, still to come, looms like a marathon.

A glass case displays hot dogs turning on rollers. I'm tempted. But my head is already giving me trouble. No use adding my stomach to the list of challenges.

I wander the aisles, looking for something to want. I pass soup cans, cereal boxes, and thirty different kinds of chips. The end cap displays energy drinks, energy bars, and energy-boosting vitamin packets. Clearly, someone besides me needs help going the distance.

I give up and get in line with my pills. The cashier is one of the heaviest women I've ever seen. She's wearing a short-sleeved smock, and her triceps hang in huge, swaying flesh pockets. A half-eaten doughnut sits on a napkin next to the register. I put the bottle of acetaminophen on the counter without meeting her gaze. Instead, I stare at the remnants of her doughnut. Chocolate frosting. Sprinkles. My stomach turns.

I just want to go home.

When I step back into the night, the rain is gone. My legs move like they're trapped in amber. To distract myself, I try to think about the Mason case, but I can't focus. Like pieces from different puzzles, the facts don't form a coherent picture. Do I know anything for certain? Yes. Walter Mason cheats on his wife. But I guessed that much during my first interview with Kelly Mason.

The people on Kelly's list are not nice people. No surprise—people are assholes. But even if they're not involved, they all look like villains to me. Hidden agendas everywhere. There isn't one of them I'd have a drink with.

I take that back. I'd drink with Mo Brown.

I'm not sure he'd drink with me.

The closer I get to Old Town Plaza, the louder the noise gets. By the time I step out of the alley, I find myself in the middle of a maelstrom—people running in every direction, some crashing into each other. The noise is deafening. The same trash can is back on its side, burning again, smoke rolling toward the stone fountain. On the right side of the plaza, a cluster of protesters shout in unison, fists in the air. They keep repeating a phrase, but I can't understand the words. They might as well be chanting underwater.

The sound of breaking glass announces damage at the bakery. Again.

This night looks different to me. I've walked through these protests before. If someone gets too close, I square up, no problem. But tonight I'm nursing the mother of all headaches, and if I get hit, I'll go down.

I make my way to the row of businesses adjacent to my home. Someone rushes past, and I freeze in place, shoulders hunched. More footsteps behind me. I flinch.

My mouth is dry. I gasp for breath. I'm trembling. I know this feeling. I used to get it when my pops was drinking. I had it when I caught my wife cheating.

Somehow, I reach the jagged edge of the bakery window. I put my back to the shop and continue sliding left, keeping the protestors in front of me. The entrance to my apartment is in sight, but the door is blocked by two men dressed in dark hoodies. I can't see faces.

Heart pounding, my hand slips into my jacket pocket, grasping the acetaminophen. I wish I'd taken some before leaving the store. And I wish the pill bottle was a handgun.

I close on the two men. "Hey, guys," I say, struggling to make my voice sound normal. "Can I get by?" I point at the door.

The men glance at each other. One shrugs. The other steps aside. We are silent as I put my key in the door. I pull on the handle, but the man on my left still blocks me with his body. "How about a little space?"

He doesn't move for a moment, then steps aside.

"What happened to your melon?" the other man asks.

I don't answer. As I step inside the building, the back of my shoulders crawl, waiting for a blow from behind that doesn't come.

Upstairs, I take four pills and ease myself onto the bed. Sasha watches as if I've lost my mind. I have. Lost it on the pavement in one of the alleys that leads to the plaza. You'd think a good hard blow to the head would knock sense into me. You'd be wrong.

"Time for bed, Sasha." She doesn't move. "I mean it, girl. I need more sleep."

But I can't fall asleep. The noise outside lasts until well after midnight. I try to read. I walk around the apartment. I drink glasses of water and go to the bathroom twice. Nothing helps.

At three a.m., I take Sasha outside again. The crowd is gone. Smoke, embers, and broken glass mark the plaza.

Later, when the morning sun climbs above the horizon, I finally drift off.

Chapter Nineteen
A Night Visitor

"A man can do what he wants, but not want what he wants."
~Arthur Schopenhauer

When I wake up again, another day has passed. I apologize to Sasha for my negligence and take her outside. This time, I remember the plastic bags. When we reach the alley, I scoop her previous poop, along with other piles littering the pavement around the dumpster, a kind of penance. I would keep going but bending over makes my head hurt.

The sun is setting over the mountains. It's not raining, but the last few nights have been wet. No haze in the sky—the wildfires are out. That's good. Nothing like smoke and orange skies to make you feel like Armageddon is at hand.

I feel marginally better today. Resting did me good. The prescribed two weeks of inactivity, however, is out of the question. I have cases to work. I resolve to make myself as presentable as possible and hit the road.

But after one look at my face in the community bathroom mirror, I'm horrified by what I see. My resolution to work dissolves like a January diet. I clean my wounds and ditch the head bandage, preferring to bleed into my hair.

I had wanted to follow Zoey again. She might be the key to everything, and with a little patience, I could unravel the secret to this maze. Instead, I sit at the desk, poking my cellphone, searching social media profiles, which is a different kind of maze entirely. I do name searches. I kill time.

A knock at the door makes me glance at the clock. Eight-thirty. Too late for business. My money is on Billotte. Or the crowbar killer, come to finish the job. I stand, swaying in place until my head clears. Then, I cross the room and open the door.

Kelly Mason.

I'm surprised. She looks shocked too, and I realize my face has given her a scare. "Come in," I say, stepping back.

She looks soaked. The sound of thunder makes me glance at the window. Rain pelts the glass. I hadn't noticed the storm.

She's not wearing a coat. Her yellow dress clings to her body like a second skin. Her hair, unpinned for once, hangs around her shoulders, damp and disheveled. The office light shines in her eyes. They're wet with rain, or with tears. She's never looked lovelier.

"What happened to you?" she asks.

"I got jumped the other night. A lot of nonsense goes on here." I wave in the general direction of the plaza.

"I saw all the people on my way in. A bit frightening."

"Not really," I say. "They keep the doors locked at night. How'd you get through the door, by the way?"

"Someone was coming out. I came in."

"Clever. Next time you come by, call my cell. I'll come down and let you in."

She nods, her hands clasped in front of her. Lightning flashes in the window behind me, and the rain intensifies.

"You should sit down. Where's your jacket?"

She sits in one of my two client chairs. The right one. "I left the house without it. I was. . . upset."

"I'd offer you a drink, but all I'm all out of soda. Haven't had time to get to the store. I have some liquor—"

"Whiskey, if you have it. Neat."

I watch her shiver in the chair, her arms crossed over her chest. I grab a couple of semi-clean glasses and pour two fingers for each of us. I set her glass down and turn away. Sasha is scratching at the half-room door, so I let her in the room.

"Who is this?" Kelly asks. Sasha shoves her nose in Kelly's lap. She unfolds and pets my pup.

"Her name is Sasha." Kelly fingers the stump of an ear, so I offer an explanation. "She's a rescue dog."

"Poor thing," Kelly says. "Do you know what happened to her?"

"Somebody cut her up. Slit her vocal cords, too. I found her in an alley. Took her to the vet, and she's been mine ever since."

Kelly looks up, horrified. "What kind of person would cut an innocent animal?"

"People are bad."

Now she's staring at me. She reaches for her glass and takes a sip, wincing.

"Sorry. I'm all out of the smooth stuff." I knock back my drink. No wincing for me. "So, what chased you out of the house without a jacket?"

"My husband got another call tonight." Her gaze fixes somewhere over my shoulder, and her lip trembles.

"Tell me."

"I heard him talking on his cellphone in the bathroom. I stood outside the door. I don't think he knew I was there. It was obvious he was being threatened. He kept trying to talk, but he was getting interrupted, because he never got in a full sentence. When the call ended, Walter stayed in the bathroom. I think . . . I think he was crying." Kelly wipes her eyes. Her shoulders are shaking.

I tell her, "Take a moment to breathe."

"Thank you." Her voice is a whisper.

I mark the time by staring at the Cave of the Winds clock. I visited that cave twice, which means I went through the entrance twice. The painting on the clock face doesn't look like the entrance I remember. Either the painting or my memory is mistaken.

"My husband is not an emotional man," Kelly says at last. "He's a good man, but he can't show emotion. I never hear him cry." She pauses, close to tears again. "I'm afraid, Mr. Ferguson. I think they're going to kill him."

I refill my glass. "What do you want me to do?"

"I came here hoping you'd follow Walter and protect him if someone tries to hurt him." She sits back, staring at my head. "Is that something you could do?"

I know what she's thinking. Same thing she was thinking when she first came into my office. *Can this guy really do the job?* I'm tempted to argue my cause, but what's the point? I'm wearing the counter argument on my face.

"Are you going to let me talk to Walter about this?"

"No, you *mustn't*. I don't want him to know." Her expression seems genuinely stricken.

"You understand that protecting him would be easier if I could talk to him, right?"

She looks away. I'm not going to win this argument.

I tap the wound on the side of my head, more out of nervousness than anything else. "You're worried about your husband. But not worried enough to tell him I've been hired to protect him?"

"You don't understand."

"You're right," I say. "I don't understand."

"We're. . . not doing well right now."

"No shit. He's cheating on you." There's anger in my voice, and it surprises me.

She won't meet my gaze. "I suppose you're wondering why I stay with him."

"I told you, I understand the issue of infidelity. My ex was a cheat. And I'm not divorced because she cheated. I'm divorced because she left me. I might have given the marriage another shot. So, I'm certainly in no position to judge you."

Ignoring my confession, she continues. "I'm trying to explain why I don't want him to know I've hired you. There are things in our marriage that are kept separate. A pragmatic choice on both our parts. He has his imperfections, and I certainly have mine."

"Are you cheating on him, too?" I ask.

She blushes a deep red. "No, of course not. But no one is perfect, and no marriage is perfect. We've. . . compartmentalized certain things, so we can continue in our day-to-day lives."

I watch her as she speaks. What is it about her face? Is it the curve of her lips? The shape of her brows? She sits shivering in my chair, looking half-drowned, and I'm thinking she's the most beautiful woman I've ever seen. More beautiful, even, than the reserved, pinned-up version of her that first entered my office weeks ago—the one that took my breath away.

I clear my throat. "You didn't tell him about the photos."

She blushes again. "No."

"At our last meeting, you said this wasn't the first time he'd cheated. Is there an ultimatum on the table? One more slipup and he's out?"

"No." The tremor in her voice matches the misery in her eyes.

"He doesn't know that you know. About any of it?"

She closes her eyes.

"And if he did?"

She's crying now.

"If he did," I continue, "then you'd have to do something about it. You'd have to leave him."

She shrugs, tears rolling down her cheeks.

"And if he knows you hired a private eye?" There, I said it. Not security. Private investigation.

"He'll suspect I know everything," she says.

I retrieve my box of Kleenex and slide it across the desk. I blew my nose a few days ago—otherwise, Minnie is the only other person to use a tissue. I'm pleased to see the investment is finally starting to pay off. "I'll stay in the background," I promise. "He won't find out you hired me." I pause. "Has it occurred to you that having everything on the table might actually work in favor of your marriage? He's obviously hurting you. Wouldn't he be more likely to stop if he found out what you know?"

Kelly has some control of her voice back. "No. He limits himself because he doesn't want to be caught. If he knew I'd forgiven him without having ever said a word, he'd take it as an *understanding*."

Anger creeps back into my voice. "If that's so, what the hell do you want him for?"

"I love him. That's all I can say." She takes another tissue. "Let me ask you a question. How did you find out your wife was cheating?"

"I came home early. Caught her getting a throat full."

She frowns, perhaps because of my crass answer. She asks, "So you were certain. You knew for *sure*."

"Not much room for *this isn't what it looks like*."

"Afterward, when you talked about it, were you honest with each other?"

"I suppose so. Lots of shouting, but it was honest shouting."

"And did your honesty save the marriage?" Her voice has a sarcastic edge.

"Does it look like it?"

We're quiet for a few moments. I'm content to let her break the silence, and she eventually does. "I don't imagine you think very highly of me, Mr. Ferguson."

"You're wrong."

"I don't know why it matters to me, but I want you to understand. I love my husband, and the one thing I'm sure of is that he loves me. But he needs something more... more than I can give him. He has a hole inside, and he's never going to fill it."

"What does that do to you?" I ask.

She closes her eyes again.

Am I crazy? This woman must be playing me, but I cannot figure out her angle. One thing she's said rings completely true—she loves Walter. I believe that much. Whatever I imagined or hoped for, this is what I get. Drinking whiskey in my office is as close as I'm going to come to her and her world. She's a rich woman with a dicey husband, and I'm the hired help. She might as well be from Mars. Or Los Angeles.

I'm fine with that. Really. But she's in trouble, and she's scared. I'd like to help her.

"Okay," I say. "How much coverage am I going to provide your husband? I don't think you need to have him watched at work. They have building security. The only way in is through a metal detector. Shall I follow him after work? On the way to work?"

"He goes out to lunch, too."

"Lots of coverage."

"Will this cost me more?"

I put on a sad face. "I'm afraid so." More money for the hospital bill, I guess. "What about when he's home?"

"We have a home security system, so I think we're fine at home."

I don't think too much of home security systems, but I keep my mouth shut. I have to have time for shuteye, and not protecting Walter at home means I can sleep nights. There's the issue of my concussion to worry about. I can hear Corrin's voice in my head, telling me to rest.

Sorry. No rest for the wicked, Nurse Corrin.

"I have a question," she continues. "If someone thinks they're being followed, they probably aren't, right? A professional would never let himself be spotted."

"He won't spot me, if that's what you're worried about."

She grabs her glass and takes another sip of whiskey. Wincing again, she says, "You are a poor judge of whiskey, sir."

I chuckle. "Every decision is a tradeoff. This isn't the best whiskey that money can buy. But it's the best whiskey *my* money can buy." The last few minutes have been uncomfortably tense, and it's good to have some of the pressure slide away. "Out of curiosity, where does your husband think you are now?"

"I left him a note on the table, saying I needed to buy some milk."

"Better come home with milk," I advise. "Better hope there's not a full carton in the refrigerator."

"There isn't," she says. "I took it with me."

I burst out laughing, which hurts my head. Sasha barks, trying to join in. Kelly turns to look at Sasha, who has dragged a blanket into the room and curled up on it. "She seems like a very happy dog."

"She's in good hands," I tell her.

Her expression becomes serious, and she says, "I believe that's so. My husband, too? Will he be in good hands, Mr. Ferguson?"

"Call me Slag."

She shakes her head. "Never," she says.

Chapter Twenty
Back to the Hospital, Part One

"Most of us women like men, you know; it's just that we find them a constant disappointment."
~Clare Short

After Kelly leaves, I try to sleep, but I've flipped the clock. I'm awake when someone knocks at the door again. This time, it's Billotte. He has a brown bag in his hand, which he holds out to me as a gift. Inside, I find a bottle of acetaminophen and two doughnuts. One has a bite missing.

"Somebody bit this doughnut."

"Really?" Billotte asks with false surprise.

"I hope you got a price break."

Billotte walks in as if we were roommates. He plops down on my chair and puts his feet on the desk. "How's your head?"

"Better," I say. Short answers are good. No additional explanation necessary. "Thanks for the meds."

"Of course. I'd have brought them over last night, but—"

"Wait. Aren't you supposed to be working?"

At that, Billotte's expression turns. "I'm not working there anymore."

"What happened?"

"The usual." He sighs.

"You have a problem with authority."

I'm taunting him with his own line from two days earlier, but he doesn't seem to remember. "I know I do," he says. "Believe me, I had a come-to-Jesus with myself, and it's not going to happen again any time soon."

"Any time soon?"

He shrugs. "History tells me it will happen again eventually."

I grab my bottle and splash whiskey in the two glasses already on the desk. "You particular about your glassware, or should I wash these?"

"Whose germs?"

"Mine and Kelly Mason's."

Billotte raises an eyebrow.

"Working her case is running me in a circle. I was a security guy doing an investigation. Now that I've decided to certify as a P.I., I'm back to security work."

Billotte tilts his head, frowning. "How so?"

"She wants me to protect her husband."

"What are you going to do? Scare the bad guys off with your face?"

"Don't smart off to your boss."

Billotte's gaze narrows, then he smiles. "You're hiring me?"

"Part time. Temporary. Don't count on this long-term." Billotte shrugs, but I can see he's ignoring my admonition. "I'm serious, Bobby. Part time. We need to follow Walter around and make sure no one jumps him. And he can't see you, or know he's being followed."

"Why is that?"

"Long story. Can you do it? Walter goes to and from his job and goes out for lunch and meetings. I can't cover everything. Can you help me?"

"What are you going to do if someone attacks him?"

I try for a serious expression. "There's not much *I* can do. My head's killing me. But if someone attacks Walter while you're on the job. . .you'll have to take a bullet."

"Ha. Funny. When do I start?"

I consider this. How can he best help me? "I'll watch him going to and from his job. Morning and evening. But I'm worried about lunchtime. That's when I've been sleeping."

"Okay. What do I do?"

I spend the next half hour explaining how to tail Walter without being spotted. At first, I'm struck by the absurdity of this. On-the-job training shouldn't include whiskey. But Billotte isn't acting like Billotte—he seems calm and inquisitive, soaking up the information. I keep waiting for his eyes to glaze over, but they don't.

I finish by explaining the location of Walter's office and his make of car. "Find his car in the lot first."

"When does he go to lunch?"

"It varies. Get to the parking lot by ten. Plan to stay at least until three or four."

"Ten in the morning?"

"Lunchtime happens during daylight hours, Bobby. And he sometimes leaves the office for meetings in the afternoon. You'll be working most of each day. Starting tomorrow."

"How do I follow him?"

"You have a license, right?"

"License to kill." Bobby cracks wise at the wrong time. (I would never do that.)

"License to drive. Do you have one?"

"Of course."

"You'll drive Betsy." Billotte gives me a blank look. "My car." I slide a spare key across the desk. "You know where I park, right?"

"What kind of moron names his car Betsy?"

"Your boss does."

"Right." He scratches his chin, which has never, to my recollection, had a whisker on it. Baby-faced Italian. "This would be a whole lot easier if Walter had a schedule."

I almost change my mind, then. Billotte can't really help me, and if he behaves like himself, he might cause serious problems. But my head hurts. Besides, no one is going to put a hit on Walter Mason in the middle of the day in the middle of Old Town Westbrook. Billotte will simply be another set of eyes so I can close mine.

* * * * *

The worst thing about sleep deprivation isn't being tired. I've worked late nights for years. I'm used to that. But climbing into bed and *not* sleeping takes an incredible amount of effort. Tossing, turning, stretching, adjusting blankets, and apologizing to your dog takes energy. Trying to lie still can be painful. And the futility of willing yourself asleep leaves you utterly drained.

The night passes, one tick of the clock at a time. I spider my way through social media profiles, looking for a clue I haven't noticed before. When that game begins to pale, I read news sites, keeping myself up to date with current events, none of which seems to apply to my life or the lives of any of my friends. We work for a living. We worry about bills. We worry about getting the laundry done. We don't worry about politics—that privileged world strikes me as insane.

As morning approaches, I get ready for my first day as Walter's bodyguard. I take care of Sasha's needs and hop into Betsy. I park a half block from Walter's house one hour before the sun rises.

I check the other cars on the street for potential threats. Walter's home is a red zone. Anyone planning to hurt him might well stage here. The space between his front door and his car, parked at the curb, is vulnerable. I imagine myself picking a spot to attack Walter from. I would need a clear line of sight, a place to hide, and a way out when the damage was done. I get out of my car and walk around, not worrying about being spotted. If someone is here, already planning to hurt Walter, seeing me might well put him off the job.

The Mason home is in an older part of Westbrook. Beautiful brick or sandstone homes. No garages, but plenty of trees and shrubs. Hiding places. I surveille the area. One little copse of pines sitting next to an alley looks like a promising attack spot. Empty. Satisfied that Walter is safe—for the moment—I return to my car.

When the butt crack of dawn arrives, Walter walks to his car and drives away.

I follow him to the municipal building parking lot. He's less likely to meet trouble there. Once he's inside, I drive away, pleased that I'm one breakfast sandwich away from bed.

* * * * *

I walk Sasha at three in the afternoon. When I return to the office, Billotte is there waiting. "You're supposed to be watching Walter," I say, irritation in my voice.

I fish for my set of keys, so I don't really notice his face. Once we're inside, I get a glimpse, and it scares me. "What's wrong?" Billotte's face blanches at the question.

"Bad news, man."

"What happened. Is Walter okay?"

A momentary flicker in his eyes tells me I need to shut up.

"Walter's fine. Fat and happy. But Minnie isn't."

Minnie.

"Santiago paid her a visit last night. She's in the hospital."

I don't say a word. I cross the room to my desk and sit. Outside, the air is cool and crisp, but the office is stifling. Hot and musty with the odor of man and dog. When I speak, my voice chokes with anger. "Can you go back and follow Walter home? I need to go to the hospital."

"Yeah, I can do it." Billotte watches me closely. "Hey? There's one more thing." He digs into his back pocket and pulls out a sheet of paper, folded and crumpled.

"What's this?"

"Walter's schedule for the week."

I unfold a computer printout, careful not to tear it. "Where did you get this?"

"From his receptionist. Simone. Nice girl."

I leave the office, shaking my head.

* * * * *

I go to the emergency room first, but they've already moved Minnie to another room. In the ER lobby, I see Corrin talking to a family. She sees me, too, and pauses in her conversation. She probably thinks I'm here to get my face fixed.

I give thought to grabbing a vase of flowers at the gift shop, but I decide not to. I'm here to apologize to Minnie. I promised her I wouldn't fuck up, but I did fuck up, and she took the brunt of it. Flowers won't do.

Her room is on the second floor. By the time I wander the labyrinth of halls and locate her room, Minnie is sitting up in her bed, waiting for dinner. The curtains are closed, and the lights are low. Even so, I can see the damage to her face. Half of her head is bandaged. The machine she's hooked to clicks once and goes silent as the room. I stand still. She's not speaking.

Finally, she asks, "What happened to your face?" Her voice garbles, as if her mouth is full of pebbles.

"I got jumped in an alley."

"Was it Santiago?"

"I don't think so. Might have been his crew, or it might have been someone else. I make friends all over town." She does not smile. My joke falls as flat as my wretched heart.

I react to stress and tragedy with jokes. Some people call it "gallows humor," but I shouldn't make light of Minnie's tragedy to relieve my tension. There's nothing funny about this. My wit serves a world without smiles.

I apologize, both for the joke and for underestimating her dilemma. "I'm so, so sorry."

Her voice slurs. She has mouth damage. "You didn't charge me. Otherwise, I'd be asking for a refund."

She's got better jokes than I do.

"Santiago?" I ask.

She nods.

"Did you tell the police?"

She shakes her head no. "They think someone broke in and attacked me. There are a lot of people from out of town here for the demonstrations. I blamed them."

"Why?"

She doesn't answer at first. She's probably thinking, after all that's happened, I haven't learned a thing. "If I make a report, the police will talk to him and do nothing. A day or two later, I'll be back here, or in a box." She pauses, prodding her puffy face with her fingertips. "Was a time, I thought I had this coming."

I sit down in a corner chair. My mouth stays shut.

"A long time back, he came home wanting a beer. I didn't have any in the fridge, and I got a slap for that. Next day, I bought him a six-pack. Same six beers been in my fridge ever since. He didn't want beer. He wanted to slap someone. My fool self, I thought it was my fault for not having beer when he wanted it."

"And now?"

"Beatings don't have nothing to do with beer."

I nod. "I admire you. Some folks never figure that out." I lean forward, hands on my knees. "Is there anything I can do for you?"

Her snorting laugh looks like it hurts.

Guilt is a deplorable emotion, rivaled only by pity for its sheer ugliness. But I need to embrace the feeling. I won't let myself off the hook. I misjudged Minnie's situation, and she paid the price. I swallow once, then say, "I failed you."

"That's okay. I didn't really think you'd be any help."

I almost tell her I'm going to fix things. That I'm going to solve the problem. But the last thing she needs is another promise from me. Buy her a gun? If she shoots him, they'll have her in a cell before she can blink. Help her move out of town? I think her hospital bill will follow her, even if Santiago doesn't.

Her nurse arrives with a dinner tray. A cup with straw. Two small tubs of cherry Jell-O. The nurse fusses with the little table that rolls close to the bed, placing dinner within reach. After she leaves, I ask Minnie, "You like Jell-O? I hate the stuff."

She pats her cheek. "I have some broken teeth," she mumbles. "I can suck the Jell-O down."

Are there any blunders my mouth can't manage? I sigh. "I'm going to leave now. I just wanted to see how you were, and maybe . . ." I stand, shaking my head. "I'm so sorry," is all I can manage.

I pause at the door. "I will speak to Santiago again if you want me to."

"Don't, please. Just leave it."

"All right," I say. And I leave her alone with her broken teeth.

Chapter Twenty-One
The First of Two Phone Calls

"It is dangerous to be right in matters on which the established authorities are wrong."
~Voltaire

It's just before dawn, and I'm following Walter again. He drives like an old man—hunched face-forward, peering over the steering wheel. Betsy has the slowest gas pedal in Westbrook, but I'm struggling not to run up over his bumper. It's cold this morning, and I am the kind of tired that makes my head feel like cast iron. I change my breathing, my sitting position, and blink my eyes—anything to stay awake. Once Walter is inside the building, I head home. I need rest.

I was knocked out in my last Golden Gloves fight. I woke up on the canvas, staring at the lights and the shadows of men. Garbled sounds came as if filtered through water. Gradually, I was able to focus on the ref and hear him ask if I was okay.

That is how I wake up each day since someone used my head as a piñata.

Which also explains why I've forgotten something important to me. I was supposed to box with Manny and Lee today. I slept through it without thinking. Hard to tell what day it is when your mile markers are moved.

I grab my cellphone and call Manny. He answers on the fourth ring. "Slag?" I launch into an apology, but Manny cuts me short. "I don't think it's a good idea for you to come around here for a while. Everyone at the center thinks you jumped Santiago Alvarez."

"That's not true," I say. There's no answer, so I ask, "Do *you* think I jumped him?"

At first, no answer.

"Manny?"

"I wasn't there." He pauses. "But no. I don't believe it. Not that my opinion matters to everyone down here."

"What are they saying?" Then, "Never mind. I don't give a shit what they think. I care about you. We're good, right? You and I?"

"We're good." No hesitation. "But you ought to stay away for a while."

I sigh. "Okay. We will pick up the boxing where we left off sometime down the road. Until then, take care of yourself."

"Watch your back," he says.

I hang up and slump into my desk chair. I feel like I'm down for an eight count. I have dozens of acquaintances but only a handful of friends. I think of Manny as one of the latter. I retrace our conversation, including that first pause, and the words, "I wasn't there." He didn't see Santiago pull the knife. How could he know for sure? I've asked Manny to side with me against his friends and neighbors. Maybe that's asking too much.

Then again, no it isn't. Manny is a smart kid. I've been sparring with him for six months. He knows my temperament. He knows my character. In the ring, you can't hide who you are.

His friends and neighbors? They don't know me.

Still, those friends and neighbors are important to him, and they think I'm the bad guy. They think I'm a thug. Maybe I'm a racist. I close my eyes. Whether it's my concussion or my sad world, something is making me sick to my stomach. Making me want to hit someone.

* * * * *

The weather turns for the worse. By the time the sun sets, the sky is black and wet. Rain chases everyone away, leaving the plaza quiet and empty. Sasha shivers to let me know our walk should be short. I stay close to the shops, letting the overhangs and awnings shield us from what is becoming a downpour. Raindrops dance on the pavement stones. The boom of thunder makes us both flinch. Our coats are soaked.

Billotte is, once again, covering for me. I am too weak to work. Still, my brain is putting in overtime, trying to tie the different threads of this case together. How does it all fit?

Or does it?

Then, just like in the movies, the phone rings, interrupting a moment of quiet despair. I duck under an awning, my back to the building, and pull out my cell.

Lloyd. My buddy, the cook. I surprise myself with how happy I am to hear from him. "Lloyd! What's up? How are you?"

"I'm okay."

"You working?"

"No. Downtown Chicken is done. That's why—"

"Have you put out any applications?"

Pause. "Yeah, I applied at the Italian joint north of the plaza, but they didn't interview me."

"Make sure you go back. They'll hire you. The manager is an asshole, and he always needs help."

"I hate Italian food," Lloyd says. "Pasta makes you fart. Anyway, that's not why I'm calling."

"You don't need a reason to call, you know."

"I know. But listen—this is important. You're always asking me about Mo Brown, and I didn't know if you heard, so I called."

"Heard what?"

"Somebody shot him. In the restaurant. He was there late last night, and somebody shot him."

"Is he dead?"

"I don't think so. I think he's in the hospital."

"Well, that's messed up."

"You're telling me." Pause. "I don't think regular bullets can kill that guy."

Did Walter Mason shoot Mo Brown? Not likely. I think of Walter's tight shoes and his tiny, mincing steps, and I don't think he could face Mo Brown in person.

Did he hire someone to do his business?

"Lloyd, I've gotta go. Thanks for the info. Listen, we need to get together in a few days. I'm buying. Be nice to sit together on the same side of the bar for once."

"That sounds good to me." He sounds sincere.

"Talk to you," I say, and hang up.

The bakery is closed. No newspaper for me. I stay where I'm at, back against the wet building, cellphone in hand, and search online for a news story. *Nothing.* When they closed Mo's restaurant, stories and features appeared like magic. Now, Mo takes a bullet, and nothing. Not a word.

Lloyd might be wrong, which would explain the silence. I take Sasha to the apartment, dry her off with a towel, and head to my car. Betsy and I are going to the hospital.

As I drive, I try to wrap my head around Mo Brown as a victim. I can't believe Walter would have him shot. That's tin foil hat thinking. Maybe Mo's connections back east didn't like having their restaurant closed. Maybe Mo pissed off an ex-employee or a jealous husband. Or a girlfriend.

When in doubt, blame a woman.

I park near the hospital entrance and go inside. After a brief detour, I approach the front desk. The receptionist is a young man in a blue smock. He asks who I'm visiting. "Maurice Brown. They told me he was shot."

"Oh, yes." He pecks away at his computer and looks up. "I'm sorry, are you related? I can only let immediate family in."

I lean in close, my palms on the counter. "Mo is my brother."

The receptionist frowns.

"I'm Mark Ferguson. I kept my father's name. Mo kept his mother's name. It's complicated. The new American family and all." I inch closer. "Which room?"

"May I see some identification, please?"

I open my wallet and pull out my driver's license. Sure enough, I'm Mark Ferguson.

* * * * *

In the movies, the patient awakens to find a loved one who spent the night in a chair next to the bed. If the patient has been in a coma, the loved one has been there for days or weeks, reading passages from *Moby Dick* and stroking hands.

Mo wakes up to me. "What the fuck?" he asks.

I should call a nurse, but I want a moment alone. The staff will come soon enough, and I'll be sent out of here.

Mo is cradled in a nest of wires. The bed is too small for him, and his feet stick out on either side of the metal bed frame. His eyes flutter as he looks around. Then, his gaze comes back to me. "What the fuck?" he asks again. An appropriate question both times.

"Hello, Mo."

"You here to finish me?"

I blink. "Oh, hell no. I'm Slag Ferguson, remember? I'm a good guy. Private investigator. I heard someone shot you, so I came to see how you are."

"Who let you in here?" he demands, his face contorted, either from pain or from anger.

"I told them I was your brother."

His face goes blank, and then he bursts out laughing, followed immediately by another grimace. Pain, then. When he speaks, he pushes the words out in short bursts. "My brother? You'd be a tiny skeleton tied to a rock." He paused to take a breath. "They'd find you at the bottom of Delaware Bay. Get me a drink."

"Smart to kill me early on," I tell him. "I tend to grow on people, otherwise."

There's a cup and straw on the table next to the bed. I hold it out so Mo can sip. Then, he pushes his big head back into his pillow. "What are you doing here?"

One of the machines is beeping. An alert? Who knows? I probably don't have much time. I lean forward and say, "I was hired by Walter Mason's wife to find out who's blackmailing him. You're a natural suspect, given what's going on. Can you tell me something that will clear things up?"

"Why should I?"

"Because I brought you flowers." I point to the sad little vase I've set on the table next to him.

Mo starts to laugh again, then forces himself to be still.

A nurse strides into the room, a sour expression on her face. I'm afraid my time might be up. "Mr. Brown? How are you feeling?" Then she looks at me, frowning. "Hello. Are you family?"

"I'm his brother."

Mo nods. "He's the ugly one in the family."

The nurse gives Mo a condescending smile and takes his vitals, glancing at me every few moments. When she leaves, promising to return with meds and a doctor, I turn back to Mo. "Does it seem strange to you that they let me in your room? You were shot. I'm not complaining, but why would they let me in here?"

"You're the private dick. You can't figure it out?" He pauses to suck air. "The po-po don't offer. . . private security services. They'll send a detective over and ask me . . .a few questions. That'll be it. Otherwise—"

"You have a lot of enemies." Mo's chest is covered in bandages. "How many shots did you take?"

"Three, I think. One in the shoulder. One in the thigh."

"I think someone in Health and Environment is shutting down your restaurant to make room for a new Community Center."

"You said that the last time."

"You might be trying to hit back by blackmailing Walter Mason. I don't believe it. But it occurred to me that your business partners could be doing the dirty work. You might not even know."

He doesn't say a thing, so I continue. "Either way, Walter Mason is the villain here. Armando de San Martín, too. So, if you *are* blackmailing Walter, I don't blame you. But knowing for sure would help me put Mrs. Mason's mind at ease."

"Laying here in bed full o' holes, that's the thing . . .I'm most fucking worried about." Mo shakes his head slowly from side to side. "If I could get up, I'd bust your head."

"I knew you being laid up was my best chance to start a friendship."

Again, I've caught him off guard. A smile twitches at the corners of his mouth. "You don't know shit."

"Enlighten me."

"You already got the general idea. They're trying to take my restaurant. That's obvious enough. But you haven't figured out who's . . .wearing which hat."

The nurse reappears, doctor in tow, and he's not happy. "Excuse me. Do you have permission to be here?"

"I'm his brother."

The doctor looks at Mo, then at me. "Pardon my skepticism."

I consider calling him a racist, but I can use my limited time better than that. I turn to Mo. "You aren't blackmailing Walter for cheating on his wife?"

Mo scowls. "I told you already . . .no."

Then it hits me like a tire iron from behind. I think I know how the pieces fit. "One last thing. Do you have first right of refusal on the sale of your restaurant?"

Mo gives me an ugly smile. The smile of a predator. Wounded but still dangerous. "Now you're cooking."

"I'm sorry, but you have to leave," the doctor says. The nurse stands behind him, nodding in agreement.

"I'm gone," I say. I'm down the hall before they call someone.

I realize my mistake. Just because two things are stacked together doesn't mean they're connected. In doing so, I ignored the most basic rule: *Follow the money.* Mo has the first right of refusal. His partners can't sell without coming to Mo first. If they're brokering a sweet deal with a developer, he gets a shot at the same deal.

Seeing Mo stretched out and helpless bothers me. Some people like to see the mighty brought low. That's the essence of Greek Tragedy, right? Not me. A man like Mo Brown doesn't have clean hands, but then, who does? As for his chicken shack, he built the thing from scratch, in exchange for a tiny sliver of pie. And somebody wants what's his. It's a crime.

Right of first refusal. He can complicate the transfer of ownership. But not if he's dead.

In the lobby, I run into Nurse Corrin. She has a clipboard in her hand, but she sets it on a chair when she sees me. I walk up close. She smells good. I focus on her eyes, ignoring her perplexed frown. "Here again?" she asks.

"A friend."

Her frown deepens.

"Mo Brown. You had him in surgery. He was shot." I try to look sad.

She gives me an odd look. "Seems like being your friend might be dangerous."

"Not so," I tell her. "Knowing me is a good thing." Then I think of Minnie, and I shut up.

Chapter Twenty-Two
The Way Things Work

"Governments have never learned anything from history or acted on principles deducted from it."
~Georg Wilhelm Friedrich Hegel

Morning rolls toward me like a slow-moving freight train. Still unable to sleep, I spend the night searching online for clues.

Searches will be easier when I'm certified. More databases.

By morning, I still don't have the names I want, but I have an idea of what might be going on. Walter could give me answers if I confronted him, but I've agreed to watch over him instead. I regret the promise.

On the other hand, I also promised to find out whether Walter is a straight arrow or on the take. Does one promise cancel the other?

Someone shot Mo Brown. In Westbrook. Things are getting ugly.

Before dawn breaks, I return to Walter's home address. There's no way I'm going to let him be the next victim. I park farther away than usual and walk on the dark side of the street. The earthy smell of wet, fallen leaves hangs in the cold morning air. The fact that I can smell anything is an improvement. Maybe my head is healing.

In the dark, colors mute and dampen, giving the street an odd, nostalgic feel, like an old black-and-white film. Without meaning to, I think of autumns back when I was young. In the Midwest, trees splash red and purple like a bareknuckle match. Here in Colorado, the Aspen turn the color of urine.

The air is chilly and damp, and I don't have a coat. I left the house unprepared.

I look up the road, checking the spots I've identified as likely staging areas for someone hoping to hurt Walter. A row of hedges sits forlorn and unattended. Good. Closer to Walter's house, I stop dead. Two legs have joined the tree trunks in the copse of pines across the street. Someone is standing in the shadows, backlit by a backdoor porch light.

I'm still more than a half block away and I've been padding down the street like an old man. I return to my car, hoping I wasn't spotted. I circle back to the street running parallel to Walter's, searching for the backside of the alley leading to the pine trees. When I find it, I creep along the fenced yards of houses, avoiding the noisy gravel. My heart pounds like fists on a speed bag. I am not prepared for a confrontation. I am not carrying a gun. I can't get into an extended fist fight because of my throbbing head.

Nor can I wait for Walter to be shot leaving his house.

Ahead, a man crouches, his back to me. Fifty feet separate us. A dog begins to bark, and I freeze. The man does not turn.

Slowly, now. One step after the other, barely breathing. When he hears me, and he will, I'll sprint the gap and bull rush him into the trees. Each step closer makes that plan seem more reasonable. When I'm just ten feet away, he feels me coming and turns.

Just like a movie.

He has time to stand before I hit him chest high, knocking his handgun into the trees. He bounces off a branch and steadies himself, searching for the gun. I ignore the weapon and step into him, throwing a glancing right. I get enough of his chin to drop him to his knees.

I follow with a left and send him sprawling. Walking to the pistol, I bend and reach. For a moment, I think I'm going to pass out. My left eye goes black. I grab the pistol grip and hold on. I'm not going to use the gun, but neither is he. I raise the weapon and point it where he might be standing.

I'm not sure.

In a moment, my vision kicks in again, though everything is blurry. Tears stream down my cheeks. He's on the ground, hands in the air, staring at me. He's a small fellow with an unfortunate face. Nose like a bird's beak. Ears that ought to enable flight.

He starts for his wallet. "I'm a licensed private investigator. You're making a huge mistake—"

"Shut up." Backing into the alley, I use a standard two-handed grip and aim the pistol at his face.

"You're in a lot of trouble!" he says, his voice shaking.

"Do I have to shoot you in the mouth to shut you up?" I struggle for a flat delivery. Funny lines like that work best when they're understated.

His eyes go wide, but his lips clamp shut.

"Nice hiding place you have here." I've already decided he's probably not here to kill Walter. The pistol is a .38 snub-nosed Ruger—an upscale belly gun. Pretty good for close range. For assassinating someone across the street? No way.

"I'm protecting the Mason family. And you're here to hurt them."

"Don't be ridiculous. You're the guy who brought a weapon here."

His mouth flops open again. He considers my words and says, "They've been threatened, and you're interfering. If they get hurt now, it will be on you."

"I don't think I believe you. Let's walk over, knock on the door, and see what Walter says."

He looks stricken. "No! Why would you do that? Listen, I've got identification. Let me reach for it—"

"Slow," I warn. "Toss your wallet my way. Then put your hands on top your head and shut up." He does as I ask. I worry about bending down again, but I manage. "Okay," I say after studying his credentials. "You have a cool identification card. So what?"

"It shows I'm here legitimately."

I motion him forward, and he joins me in the alley. The lights at the back of a house give me a better look at his face. In addition to that nose and those ears, his face is pocked. He probably went into investigation because he heard chicks dig private eyes, though in my experience, it's not true.

I take another glance at the card. "Reuben?"

He nods.

"Reuben, I'm going to ask you a few questions, and you're going to answer me quickly. If you pause, I'll worry that you're making up a lie. Do you understand?"

He nods again.

"Which of the Masons are you watching?"

"Until yesterday, I was following the wife. But things changed yesterday, and I was told to switch over to Mr. Mason."

"Told by whom?"

"The agency."

"Is someone else watching Mrs. Mason?"

"I don't know. I go where I'm told."

I toss the man his wallet. He sticks it in his pocket and steps closer. "Don't," I warn him. "I have one more question. Did Mrs. Mason know she was being shadowed?"

"No," he said. "We were told to be discreet."

Not too discreet. I recall Kelly asking me, "If someone thinks they're being followed, they probably aren't, right? A professional would never let himself be spotted." I give Reuben another glance. He's no professional.

Across the street, the front door closes and Walter walks out to his car like nothing could possibly hurt in his own front yard. I step out from behind the trees and wave. "Walter? Walter Mason?"

Walter freezes. He's staring at my gun hand. I point the gun at the ground. "Walter, we need to talk."

"Please," he says. "Don't." He holds his hands up, as if his palms could stop a bullet.

"Calm down, Walter. I'm not here to hurt you." I look to the pines. "Come out, Reuben," I say. "Step into the street." Then I turn back. "Walter, I found this guy hiding in the trees over here. He was armed. No need to worry. He's not armed now."

Reuben comes at me, moving fast. I hear his footsteps and have a fist waiting for him. Not a clean hit, but I bloody his nose. He staggers back on wobbly legs, trying to stay upright.

"Sit down, Reuben," I say.

He sits on the curb, his face in his hands. "That's my gun! You are in *so* much trouble."

Something occurs to me, and I suddenly burn with curiosity. "Are you certified as a private investigator?"

Reuben looks confused. "Yes."

I snort. "Money well-spent, huh?" I turn back to Walter. "You should have hired a security guard."

Walter watches, locked in place. "Who are you?"

"My name is Slag Ferguson. I'm a private investigator, hired by your wife, Kelly. And you need to get out of the street. Out in the open, you're a target."

"What?" Walter's expression makes me laugh.

"Let's walk to your car. *Now.*" I begin to move. He jumps back, flinching. "I'm not going to hurt you, damn it. But you need to get to cover."

Walter shuffles to his car. Behind us, Reuben stays seated on the curb. I open Walter's car door and he slides inside. Holding the door, I tell him, "Drive to the municipal building and wait for me in the parking lot. I'll escort you to your office and make sure you're safe."

By now, Walter has figured out I'm not going to harm him. He casts a glance back at Reuben and scowls as he starts his car.

As Walter drives away, I remove six rounds from Reuben's revolver and pocket them. Walking past, I toss the empty gun into his lap.

"Fuck you," he says. "I'm pressing charges."

I stop for a moment. "That would be stupid. You don't want your bosses to know what a pussy you are."

Walking on, I find I'm lightheaded, but otherwise feeling pretty good. I can see hints of sunshine on the horizon. By the time I reach the parking lot at the municipal building, I'm smiling and humming a tune.

I climb out of Betsy and walk over to Walter's Escalade. When I tap the passenger side window, he unlocks the door, and I slide inside. The seats are leather. Nice. He stares at my empty hands. "I gave Reuben back his gun."

"Who are you?" he demands.

I repeat my introduction. "My name is Slag Ferguson. Your wife hired me to find out who is blackmailing you."

"Blackmailing?" His voice is flat, neither denying nor acknowledging he's heard. "Do you have some credentials?"

"No. I'm not certified." My answer is a little too defensive, so I add a dash of snide. "Your boy had credentials, though. How'd that work out?"

Walter's frown deepens. "You say my wife hired you? When was this?"

"Weeks ago." Now that I'm in this conversation, I wonder how much I should disclose. I've already disregarded Kelly's wishes by talking to Walter directly. I had a good excuse, of course. Reuben was a godsend. "Your boy said he was shadowing Mrs. Mason until yesterday. I assume the switch has to do with the hit on Mo Brown?"

Walter grumbles and grips the wheel of the Escalade. "Yes."

"Why follow her in the first place?" I ask. "Are you having doubts about her?"

Walter scoffs. "Of course not."

"Okay, then. Why follow her?"

Walter thinks before answering. Bad sign? "I don't know how much you've learned about Maurice Brown's troubles in his—"

"I know the city is trying to close him down so they can relocate the Community Center."

Walter looks at me like I'm stepping off the short bus. "Don't be absurd. That corner is prime property. The city would never put a community center there."

"Mo Brown seems to think so." As do I.

Walter snorts. "Hard to convince Mr. Brown otherwise, once he has an idea in his head. The man is stubborn."

"I don't understand the city's motivation, then."

"Money, of course," he says. He exhales. He lets go of the wheel, and his hands drop down into his lap. Then he looks at me. "How much do you know? What did Mr. Brown tell you?"

"Mo is closed-mouthed about things. But he told me enough to put two and two together."

Walter pauses again. Perhaps, like me, he's wondering how much he ought to say. "Mr. Brown did not want to sell his restaurant, and I did not want to put him out of business. Both of us turned down offers. He turned down offers to buy. I turned down incentives to shut him down. And when we resisted, threats were made."

"Threats?"

"Powerful people don't take no for an answer."

"Who's wearing the black hats?" I ask.

He looks me in the eye and says, "All of them."

I've heard that line before.

"I'm going to give you a piece of advice that someone in your profession should always remember," Walter says. *"Follow the money."* He delivers this line like a magician pulling the handkerchief aside to reveal that the goldfish have escaped the bowl. Very theatrical.

"Great," I say. "So how does money change hands on a deal like this? And why would the city put a tax revenue source out of business?"

"Businesses on that corner consistently failed prior to Downtown Chicken. Mr. Brown's success threatens to raise the real value of the property. Acquiring a successful property is expensive." Walter's voice acquires a tone that isn't lost on me. He's lecturing. "If, on the other hand, an asset is sold for a price reflecting consistent failure at that location, coinciding with the apparent panic of motivated owners, and the property is then developed or resold for a premium price—a matter of timing—the profits can be extraordinary. The restaurant served the purpose of, shall we say, laundering the profits from other endeavors. Now, a more profitable purpose has arisen."

I hold up a hand. "What's the city get out of it?"

Walter sighs. "Not the city. *City officials.*" He checks his watch. He seems to be considering whether or not to continue educating me. "Look, on the simplest level, there are bribes. Any project requires multiple steps to reach fruition. Inspections. Permits. Environmental impact. Right now, it takes the city a year and a half to review blueprints for a building permit."

"So, all the little palms get greased?"

"Don't be absurd. The people who schedule and direct others get paid." He shakes his head. "The people in the field take orders."

"Bribery leaves a paper trail, doesn't it?"

Walter snorts. "Payments are more sophisticated than that. Some end up as donations to charitable organizations. People on the board of directors for those charities draw salaries. Others are paid consulting fees. Speaking fees. Relatives are hired by contractors. Inflated contracts are signed. There are a multitude of ways for money to change hands."

I shake my head. "You're overloading me, here."

Earlier, he was frightened by Reuben's gun. Now, he's in command again. Clearly enjoying the opportunity to "school" me. "Is this all new to you? The game is pay-to-play. When the rewards are huge, like the kind of development proposed for that corner, the payoffs are huge as well.

"With a project as big as this," he continues, "the deal will often include additional stipulations. For example, the developers may agree to certain projects to benefit the community in exchange for allowing the project to go forward. Affordable housing or infrastructure improvements—that sort of thing—which means additional projects benefitting both the officials *and* the developers, depending on which companies get the bids. When public housing is in the mix, there's another layer of fraud that can occur—everything from phony receipts to ghost employees. Hell, some HUD programs put cash directly in administrators' hands. The money gets used like an ATM card." Walter stops long enough to give me a condescending look. "Did you seriously not know any of this? How could you not? Are you a child?"

I'm reminded of the drunk at Wesley's—the one who mocked me for not knowing current events. This is the same thing, only worse. "What about Mo's partners?" I ask.

Walter snorts. "Running a restaurant is a slow, honest way to make a dollar. Lowballing the selling price of an asset, writing off your losses, and pocketing untaxed payoffs is big money. In this case the problem is—"

"Mo Brown has right of refusal."

Walter nods, raising a single eyebrow. I've surprised him. "The friends back east who bankrolled him wanted to keep an eye on the partners here in

Colorado. Mo was the check that kept them in balance. Once the partners made their deals, Mo was supposed to back off and close down. But he wouldn't do it. He loves that damned restaurant."

"Who shot him?" I ask.

Walter shrugged. "The boys back east? The developers? His own partners here in Westbrook? Take your pick."

"How does Armando de San Martín figure into this?"

"He doesn't." Walter seems emphatic on this point. "Mr. Brown thinks he was involved, and he was—inadvertently. Not in the way Brown imagined. The Commissioner would love for the city to move his little center downtown, but it's not going to happen."

"I saw his blueprints."

"As I told you, getting the city to okay blueprints takes forever. If you want to pitch a project, you need plans long before you ever break ground." Walter notes my expression and nods. "You're beginning to understand, aren't you? The people behind the scenes were all too happy to have the commissioner go public with his plans. Shutting down a private business is still considered bad form, unless it's for a *good cause*. But the commissioner was never really a player. He was a distraction. A bit of misdirection."

"What did he get out of it, then?"

"Nothing. His contribution was serendipitous."

"You're telling me he's clean?"

"*Grow up*. He's a *politician*. But he's got money and doesn't seem to want to pad his own nest. He's an *advocate*. He *believes* the things he says. He's had his eye on that property since the previous owner went out of business."

"So, Mo Brown is wrong?"

"There aren't any people like Armando de San Martín where Mr. Brown comes from. He doesn't know what he's looking at."

"And you? Are you clean?" I ask.

It's the million-dollar question. He's not in any hurry to answer. He tugs at his little goatee, shifting in his seat. "I'm not a believer like the commissioner," he admits.

"But?"

"But I try to do the right thing. Sometimes, it seems like there's no point, but I still try."

Except when it comes to being faithful to your wife. That's what I ought to say, but Kelly asked me to keep quiet. Still, Walter's lecture stings me. I'm not a child. Later, when this is all over, I'll research the kinds of graft he mentioned. In the meantime, I want my pound of flesh from this pompous ass.

"So, you're a good guy?" I ask.

He nods.

"Call me skeptical. I don't think you give a damn about right and wrong. You try to live up to how your wife sees you—when it's convenient."

The air goes out of him like an old toy balloon.

"You're wrong," he says.

Outside, the sun is up. The parking lot, empty when we first arrived, is filling fast. He continues with a little more conviction in his voice. "The fact is, I *do* admire Mr. Brown. He has a rough-hewn sort of integrity. I want him to keep his restaurant."

"Who is blackmailing you?"

"I'm not being *blackmailed.*" His voice shifts again. Now he's being petulant. "I'm being *threatened.* And how would I know who they are? They don't leave a name when they call." Walter shakes his head again, like I'm a slow learner.

I *am* a slow learner. But I'm getting up to speed.

"Have you complained to anyone?" *Not if he's being blackmailed.*

"Complain to whom? The police? My superiors? The mayor? How am I supposed to know who is and isn't involved?"

"What are they threatening you with?" I sincerely doubt he's going to admit to adultery, but I want to see what he says.

"They threatened to hurt my wife."

My heart nearly stops. "What? Wait a minute. What are you saying?"

"They said they'd hurt my wife if I didn't cooperate."

I stare at Walter like he's grown a second nose. "The little guy back at your house said he'd switched over to watching *you.*"

"Yes. I thought that was prudent after the attack on Mr. Brown."

"Who's watching Kelly?"

Walter scowls at the sound of his wife's first name. "I don't see how that's any of your business—"

"Let me spell it out for you. You've created gaps in your security because you keep secrets from each other. She paid me to look after you. You paid your agency to look after her. Neither one of you was aware of what the other was doing. It's like *The Gift of the Magi* for the mentally impaired."

"I suppose the situation is ironic—"

"Walter! Who is watching over your wife?"

"The agency said they'd have someone out today. Tomorrow at the latest."

I groan. "Call the agency. Tell them to get someone there *now*. I'm going to your house. I'll sit outside until your agency guy arrives. Do you have a problem with that?"

"No, no, please do, if you think it's important."

"When you call, let them know I'm outside your house. I don't want to get shot."

He looks around, agitated. "Are you going to walk me to the door?"

"What?"

"Walk me to the door," he demands.

"You're kidding." His expression says otherwise.

"Sure," I tell him. "Because holding your hand is more important than protecting your wife." I point at the municipal building. "Get inside and make the call to your agency. I've wasted enough time here as it is." I step out of the Escalade and return to Betsy. My stomach roils as I cross the parking lot. Walter will have a chat with Kelly now. She'll be angry because I talked to him, and he'll tell her how ignorant and naïve I am. Then they'll hold hands and fire me. That's how this kind of thing shakes down.

At first, Betsy won't start. I wait for a while, counting minutes, then try again. This time she fires up, and I roar out of the parking lot.

Chapter Twenty-Three
Mokroye Delo

"Every person takes the limits of their own field of vision for the limits of the world."
~Arthur Schopenhauer

The sky clouds over as I drive. I think it's going to rain again. But a storm already rages in my head. I've pushed myself today, and I ought to sleep. Instead, I'm counting the traffic lights on the way to Kelly Mason's house with a mounting sense of dread. I have butchered this case from start to finish. My ex-wife cheated on me, so I saw cheaters. Behold! I found what I was looking for. But Walter's dalliance with Zoey had *nothing* to do with what was really happening to the Mason family.

Now, everything clicks into place. Mo and Walter were, for want of a better phrase, the good guys. Walter's adultery coincided with the closing of Downtown Chicken. There was no real connection between the two. I thought I knew what was going on because Walter was a cheat, like my ex-wife. Transference? Another word for lazy and stupid.

Walter told me to *grow up*. The drunk at Wesley's—the one who'd badgered Lloyd about the Supreme Court decision—told me to *wake up*. I'm listening to them now, replaying their admonitions in my memory.

I am out of my league. Kelly trusted me. So did Minnie. They counted on the wrong guy.

Thank God for Reuben. Otherwise, I'd be the worst private investigator on the planet.

The first raindrops hit my windshield as I pull in front of the Masons' home. I turn Betsy off and try to think of what to do next. When I tell Kelly I've spoken to her husband, it's going to piss her off. Hopefully, she'll be happy to learn her husband's role in this mess doesn't involve bribery and corruption. Relieved to know that her knight's armor is still shiny.

Once I know she's safe, with the agency dick on the job, I'm going back to my apartment. I'll walk Sasha, then sleep until morning. When I wake up, my headache will be gone, and I won't give this dirty business another thought.

My eyes start to droop. I rub them with my fists and take a closer look at the house.

The front door is cracked open.

I pocket Betsy's keys and head for the door.

Pausing at the front step, I can hear the soft patter of rain on the sidewalk and street. Someone is playing music in the distance. Nothing from inside the house.

The door groans as I try to slide in through the crack. I freeze, expecting someone to slam into the door from the other side, pinning me to the frame. Doesn't happen. I step into the foyer, letting my eyes adjust to the darkness. I can't see much, but I'm not going to flick on the lights. Instead, I wait until my vision clears.

To the left, a living room. Bookshelves, furniture that matches, and paintings that don't look like they started as numbers. No television unless it's on the wall I can't see.

To the right—the kitchen. I slip across the foyer toward the light with a vague thought of grabbing a knife for defense. Not that a steak knife will mean much if an intruder is strapped. Is there even an intruder? Perhaps Kelly left the door open.

I'm not buying that.

At the entrance to the kitchen, my breath hitches. A shoe on the floor? The prep island in the middle of the kitchen blocks my view. I move one step to the left.

A foot.

I circle the island, and there she is, face down on the floor, a pool of blood under her head. I crouch down and touch the back of her neck. "It's me," I say. "Slag Ferguson. I'm here now. How badly are you hurt?" She moans. The sound is muffled by the floor. She pushes away from the blood-slicked tiles, rolling onto her side.

That's when I see what they did to her face.

* * * * *

The rest of the morning blurs. I call Walter. I accompany Kelly to the hospital with the ambulance, where I'm questioned by an actual police detective—an older man who smells like cigarettes. He asks a lot of stupid questions. Why did I go into the house? How did I know there was an intruder? What is my connection to the Mason family? What kind of record do I have? Interrogating the one person who got Kelly to the hospital is easier than actual investigating. He can tell I'm not feeling well, and when I explain that I'd been recently brained with a tire iron, he presses to find the connection between my attack and the attack on Kelly. Must be a connection, right? Like Walter's cheating and Mo's Chicken? Irony, you are a cold, stupid bitch.

Eventually, he stops talking, either because I am a dead end, or because he needs a smoke. I write out a field report, which takes forever. My eyes won't focus. Then, I use my cell app to call for a ride, suffering another freelance driver.

Finally, I am home. I give Sasha the shortest walk of her life, then plop on the bed. The next thing I know, I'm awake, and night has fallen.

* * * * *

When I leave the apartment, I run into a handful of protestors clustered near the entrance, blocking my path. I say "Excuse me," but the noise is deafening, and I am mumbling. Still, they see me, and they don't step aside.

One of the men wears a black yarn face mask. He says, "You should be out here with us." He's close enough for me to see that his eyes are green.

I ignore him.

The hospital is two miles from the apartment. I walk so I can think along the way. It's not raining, but it smells like a storm is coming. I walk fast, hands jammed into my jacket pockets. My mind keeps drifting back to this morning, showing me pictures of Kelly's face. What kind of animal would do something like that? And what kind of evil bastard would hire someone to mutilate a woman over a piece of real estate? In Westbrook? This isn't New York. This isn't Los Angeles.

I've done bad things in my life, but I can't even imagine the kind of shit I've stepped into here. Feels like I'm carrying a stomach-full of gravel. Is it guilt? Despair? My concussion? They're all intertwined.

I saw her face.

The case is closed. No loose ends left to matter. Who hit me with a tire iron? I don't know, and I don't care. Who shot Mo? Some nameless thug who's already left the city, congratulating himself over a bottle of scotch. Evil fuckers drink scotch.

As for finding the man who cut Kelly Mason's face, I tuck that away for future reference.

By the time I reach the hospital, I'm feeling plenty sorry for myself. Unemployed. Overmatched. Ahead of me is a final word with my client, who looks like Quasimodo's sister. I am sick to my stomach with dread.

But I'm no coward. I won't duck this.

When I enter her room, I find her in bed with a face full of bandages, resting like a mummy. At first, I can't tell if she's awake, but as I ease into the room, her head turns to follow. "Kelly," I say. I practiced things to say on the way to the hospital, but all I can come up with now is her name.

"Slag," she says.

"You were never going to call me that."

She's silent.

More than once, I doubted this woman. I wondered what her angle was. But she was a good person. The whole time.

I pull a chair next to her bed and sit. There's a thin brown crust at the edges of some of her bandages. In a hospital gown, with the sheet pulled to her chin, she looks frail. Her hair is tucked away behind her bandages.

"How's the food?" I ask. In this moment of agony, I can only tell jokes. I'm not funny or clever. I'm pathetic.

Again, she doesn't answer.

I sit back and close my eyes. "I'm sorry."

"What are you sorry for?"

"I should have protected you."

"That wasn't your job."

Is she blaming Walter? I open my eyes and sit forward. "Walter had someone following you. To protect you."

"I know. He told me."

"Walter was one of the good guys. Just like you said."

She draws an audible breath. "You talked to him, of course."

I nod.

"Did you happen to mention what you found out while following him? About his—"

I stop her. "No. You asked me not to, and I didn't."

Her voice is softer now. "Thank you."

I shrug, like her thanks doesn't mean that much. Like it doesn't mean the world to me. "What will you do now?"

Her head still against the pillow, she says, "I'm Walter's wife. We'll figure it out." Her words are more confident than her voice.

We are quiet then—an oddly comfortable silence. I look around the room. A single, with all the niceties. Flat screen television. Homey curtains. Walter won't skimp on accommodations. Not now.

"I'm not pretty anymore," she says, a slight tremor in her voice.

I don't think before I answer. "No, you're not. But you're beautiful."

We are quiet for a while longer. Then, she says, "I'm tired, Slag. I believe I'd like to go to sleep."

I stand. "Goodbye, then." My heart gives a lurch. I want to trace her bandaged cuts with my fingertips and tell her that no scars could ever hide who she is. Instead, I try to think of something clever. I come up dry.

"We'll speak again," she says. "Thank you for coming by."

I am being dismissed. I can only nod.

Heading down the halls, I think to peek in on Minnie. A different floor, but I have time. There's no other place I need to be. I remember the room number, though I've forgotten the correct path. I ask a passing orderly, and he directs me to the right place.

The room has two new occupants.

I check in at the nurse's station and ask for Minnie. Perhaps they've changed rooms, but no. Minnie checked out early this morning. The nurse at the computer says, "I remember her. She was a nice lady. No insurance, though. I get so frustrated when someone goes home for lack of coverage. She's required by law to have coverage, you know." She sees my expression and adds, "Poor Millie."

"Minnie," I say. "Was she well enough to go home?"

"She'll do fine, I'm sure."

"Ahhh." I have nothing else to say. I give a thought to visiting Mo while I'm here. I could go down to the gift shop and buy him one of those metallic balloons saying, *Get Well Soon!*

Or not.

On my way out, I turn down the wrong hallway, and there's Nurse Corrin talking to a family of three. She wears a serious expression. I hope no one is dying. I wait until she spots me. A perplexed look crosses her face and after finishing with the family, she comes over to say hello. "Again?" she asks.

"Another emergency," I say. "Another... friend."

"I thought you might be coming by to ask me out."

This is the kind of moment smart people would take advantage of. Serendipity with purpose. I can't muster the necessary charm "No. I came to see a friend. Someone cut up her face, and she's in her room, hoping her husband will still love her."

Silence. But I see the horror on her face.

We look at each other for a moment more, then I walk away. The automatic doors part like the Red Sea. I step out into the rain and stand still, weighing the cost of a car ride against the walk home in the cold.

I hear the door whoosh behind me, and Nurse Corrin is there. "I'm sorry about your friend. That was thoughtless of me."

"You didn't know."

"But I ought to. I should have read your expression. Sometimes, I just miss the clues."

"Me, too," I say.

"Well, see you later." She starts back inside, and adds, "You can come by just to say hello, you know."

"I will," I say, gratitude in my voice, as if I'm drowning, and someone has tossed me a life jacket. "I promise."

Walking home, I try to think about Corrin. Pretty. Clever. But thinking of her is not going to save me, so I give it up.

The heavens cut loose. Colorado isn't supposed to be a damned rain forest. Maybe the climate acolytes are right. Maybe the world is ending. I stumble through the downpour, splashing across the sidewalks. My clothes are soaked through in minutes. I feel like I'm wading through a pond. I can't breathe.

Most of the protesters are gone when I arrive. Others are still shouting in the storm. The fires are all out, but the plaza reeks of smoke.

The awning over the entrance to my apartment must really work well against the downpour, because the man in the yarn mask from earlier is still there, along with a friend. I ask them to move, but they stand still, arms folded. I stare at yarn mask for a few moments. Then I say, "I live here."

He doesn't respond.

"This is my home."

"Some people don't have a home," he says.

I take a deep breath. "I don't care. I've had a bad day, and I just want to go inside."

The man in the yarn mask isn't moving. "Do you understand what's happening here?"

"Yes, I do. I'm minding my own business, and you're in my way."

"That doesn't cut it anymore. You can't just hide and pretend nothing's happening. If you aren't with us, you're against us."

"I understand," I tell him. "What's more, I believe you." I punch him in the face. His head bounces off the door behind him before he pitches to the side, spilling onto the concrete at his feet. I turn to the friend and say, "If you don't move out of my way, I'm going to hurt you."

He steps aside without hesitation.

"Further."

He takes another few steps, leaving his friend groaning in a puddle of rain. I go inside. Adrenalin pumps through my body as I climb the apartment stairs. Instead of invigorating me, it makes me sick to my stomach.

People want to change the world. To make a difference. To give life meaning. But men and women built the world, and their natures can be read in the ruined lines of every derelict building, every patch of pavement, and every shard of broken glass. You can sort through the rubble. You can organize it into piles. But you can never clear it away.

The people in the plaza don't understand shit, and they want to tell everybody all about it. Everyone must climb onboard. Like old-time street preachers, they can't fix anything. They simply want to grow the flock.

As for me, I've had a glimpse at the gears and levers. I'm beginning to recognize how the machine works, and I don't want to talk about it anymore. I want to go to sleep.

Upstairs, I pour myself a glass of ninety-proof fuck you and stare out the window. Thinking about my two clients, Minnie and Kelly. Considering the damage. But I don't start to tear up until Sasha brushes against my leg.

I can't look down at her or pet her. I'm too ashamed.

I'd like to do one thing that isn't a punch line. I want to make something better, so that my life won't have been a useless parade of bowel movements and empty jokes.

I set my glass down on the windowsill.

The clock on the wall ticks.

Suddenly, I know what I have to do.

Chapter Twenty-Four
The Jellyfish

*"You always want to read something that everybody says has gone too far,
don't you? That's supposed to not just be charting our decline, but
embodying it?"*
~Stephen Graham Jones

The bar is small but friendly, with a row of sixteen taps, sweet-looking
waitresses that must live next door to somebody, and a central heating
system that keeps the chill of the season's first snowstorm at bay. Billotte is
excited—he's landed us a new client. Ralf Kinston has a wandering wife, and
if I can provide photographic proof, the divorce can proceed. The money is
good, though not enough for two people. Luckily, Billotte has a part-time
gig tending bar at a pinball emporium. I'm working lunch bar at an Old
Town restaurant, so we'll get by until the next round of layoffs.

I ease myself into a chair, a new habit stemming from my weeks nursing
a concussion. Billotte has a beer waiting for me, and I put half of it down
before saying hello.

"How are you feeling?" Billotte asks.

"Good. Better. I sparred this morning. First time since the attack."

"How'd you do?'

"Had a little ring rust. The kid I box with—Manny—lit me up a couple
times. He could have done more damage, but I think he was holding back.
Anyway, it was good to punch and be punched."

A musician is playing an acoustic guitar on a tiny stage in the corner. He's wearing one of those beard rings that turns his facial hair into a ponytail, but he can fingerpick the blues like a champ. His gravelly voice goes well with my beer, which I finish to the sound of his last two stanzas.

Everything is crumbling, everything is dust.
Smiling faces everywhere; you don't know who to trust.
Ain't nothin' special; it's just the Rat Town Blues.
If you got a little somethin' then you got somethin' to lose.

They talk about corruption. Talk about sin.
The one doin' the talking is the one who'll do you in.
Ain't nothin' special; it's just the Rat Town Blues.
You got a little somethin'?
Then you got somethin' to lose.

Billotte waves to get my attention. "You move out yet?" he asks.

"No. I'm beginning to wonder if they're going to evict us on schedule. The loft apartments they're building over Downtown Chicken sold fast. That might have slowed the market."

Billotte bends over a plate of wings. Placing a drummie in his mouth, he strips the meat as he pulls the bone free. "Hot," he mumbles.

The past weeks have been a struggle. My head feels better, though I worry about long-term damage. My hair grew back over the part they shaved and stitched. But my mood is black, and I don't see a way out. Putting the gloves on again helped, but not as much as I'd hoped.

I'm okay with moving from my apartment. The ongoing nonsense in the square has taken on an angrier tone. Less singing. More damage. The noise makes Sasha nervous, like every night was the Fourth of July. I think we'll both sleep better when I find a place away from the fireworks.

Mo is still recovering from gunshot wounds. Turns out there were four, not two or three, like he thought. One in the chest, one in the shoulder, and two in the thigh. The man's a bull.

I had a beer with him two weeks ago. He came into the bar leaning on a cane. Poor cane! He still thinks Armando de San Martín had something to do with what happened, but he's wrong. As Walter predicted, developers ended up with the whole block. The community center stayed where it was, though they got an upgrade to the ventilation system, courtesy of the developers. Walter was right about the city demanding side projects to seal the deal.

Mo gave me about twenty minutes. Long enough to finish a tall beer. He simmered the whole time we were together. Somebody ought to turn off the burner on that pot, but don't see it happening. Some people just smolder.

Lloyd got on at the Italian restaurant. He's doing cool stuff like curing Prosciutto, so he seems happy. We went out for shots a Friday ago, and he mentioned a girlfriend. He's never told that lie before, so I think he's really dating somebody. I couldn't be happier for him.

Walter lost his nerve, of course. Acting as the head of Health and Environment, he officially closed Downtown Chicken, and the company shut the doors forever. Walter gave interviews, citing public safety for the closure. Nobody argued. If you don't care about public health, what kind of sociopath are you? Knuckling under probably hurt his self-image, but living is preferrable to dying. I don't blame him and told him so.

I gave thought to asking Kelly Mason out for lunch, maybe to tie up loose ends, but I never called. When I talked to Walter, he said she'd already had surgery on her face. She's looking at two more procedures, bare minimum, so she prefers to stay at home. I try not to think about her much.

After my marriage fell apart, I wondered if real love exists. Kelly and Walter prove it does. But it's twisted. That kind of love makes people stupid, and it's not for me.

"So, where are we at, money-wise?" Billotte asks.

"Pickings are slim." I don't ask what he means by *we*. By now, I've given up trying to dissuade him against going down the rabbit hole with me. For better or for worse, we're partners.

"How are your classes?"

I've been pursuing certification as a private investigator, and my savings are gone. Every cent. Certification is expensive. But the classes are interesting on two fronts. First, I found out that I knew lot of the proper techniques, apparently by instinct. I appreciate the validation. Second, I had certain holes in my knowledge. *Gaping* holes. Like Swiss cheese that's mostly hole instead of cheese. I'm filling those holes. "I'm nearly finished," I say. "I'll be a licensed P.I. soon." I take another sip of beer. "You want to attend some classes?"

"Nah. Seems like work. You'll tell me what I need to know."

"You're a lazy bastard, Billotte."

He laughs.

"Anyway, I filed for a business license. We're legit. At least, I think we are. I came out of the municipal building thinking there wasn't a single person in there who understood the requirements. What authorizations I need, and such. I'm sure they'll fuck us in the end."

Billotte finishes his shot and motions to the bartender for another round. The girl behind the bar moves fast—we're known for our tips. "So, Kelly's case is closed." It was a statement, not a question.

"Yes. Not much else to do. She hired me to find out who was threatening her husband. All she really had to do was ask him. In the end, I didn't find shit."

"Can't close a case better than that."

I shut my eyes, but only for a moment. I can't afford the feelings. "I guess not."

"The government was behind some of this, right?"

I smile. "You know, there's always been crime, because crime is easier than hard work. In the old days, crime meant gangs. History's full of 'em. Then came prohibition, and that gave birth to organized crime like the Mafia. The IRS put those guys out of business. Today? We have bankers and developers working hand-in-hand with the government. Same shit. Different organizational structure."

"And Minnie's case?" Billotte asks.

I shrug and sip.

"The reason I ask is, Santiago started showing up at her door again, threatening her. Then, all of a sudden, he stopped. Minnie said she hasn't seen him in a couple weeks. She said the guys from the Community Center came around, asking about him."

"Did he take off?"

"I don't know. Minnie's got me wondering."

My next beer arrives. I thank the bartender, who is waiting tables as well, and take a sip. Billotte stares at me, unmoving. He's danced around this subject before, but I've put him off.

"I gotta tell you something," he says. "The thing is, there are lines I won't cross."

"What do you mean?"

He rubs his chin, as if thinking. Then he says, "When I was young, maybe twenty, I got into amphetamines. Way into them. I lost like fifteen pounds in two weeks because I wasn't eating. I fed most of my savings into drugs, thinking I'd quit eventually. When the money was gone, I went back to normal. Sort of. But you know what? I have no regrets. My choices, my mistakes. I probably fucked up my body a little. I might die young with a bad heart. Who cares?" He pats his belly,. "I lost some weight and I had fun."

He takes a deep breath before continuing. "But I'm a good Catholic boy, and there are some lines I just won't cross." He leans closer to me, whispering. "Please tell me you don't know what happened to Santiago."

I sip more beer, weighing my words carefully. "Santiago going away is a good thing. He was an evil prick. Minnie will be safe. Until her next relationship mistake."

Billotte considers this. "He *was* evil," he agrees. "As evil a son-of-a-bitch as I've ever met." He downs his shot and motions for another. "You mentioned the Mafia. That's something I know about. If you shoot down a capo, someone else gets promoted. If the don dies, someone else takes over the family. It isn't like cutting the head off a snake. The damned thing won't ever die. Killing a criminal isn't the end of crime. It's a job opening for another criminal."

"That's dark," I say.

"My point is you can't kill them all. You know? Evil is everywhere, and you can't wipe it out. That's the reason I'll never cross the line. It won't do any good."

"Bullshit. You won't cross that line because you're afraid for your mortal soul," I say. "And you're afraid of your mom."

"Her, too," he says.

I straighten up in my chair. I've dreaded this moment, but it had to come. Time for the truth. "You're a good Catholic boy. You said so."

Billotte nods.

"So, you understand parables?"

"Not really. I know what they are, but they can be confusing."

"You'll understand this one," I say. Then I tell him.

A man walks along a seashore. He makes his way through the sand with the help of a walking stick. As he reaches the crest of a dune, he hears a young girl's cry. Rushing ahead, he finds the sand covered with beached jellyfish. A young girl has been stung. Her father has her in his arms, and he's trying to comfort her, but she's in pain.

The man arrives and asks if there's any assistance he can offer. The father shakes his head, no. The girl wails. Welts appear on her ankles and feet.

The man looks down at the jellyfish that stung the girl and begins poking it with his walking stick, again and again, until the creature is pulped.

"It's no use," the father says. "There are a hundred jellyfish on this beach, and a thousand more waiting to be washed up on the sand. You can't kill them all."

"I know," says the man. "But I can kill this one."

Billotte reaches for his shot glass, but the liquor is gone. He looks up, blue eyes watering. "That's some fucked up shit," he says.

I search his face before answering. I want to make sure I don't say the wrong thing. Words are dangerous. "I don't think Minnie has to worry about Santi anymore."

Billotte nods. He's silent, now. I wonder if he's going to get up and walk away. Instead, he stays put, fingering his glass. He's a good friend. Loyal. "I can't do certain things," he repeats.

"I know. That's not a bad thing. One of us should have a moral compass."

Billotte smiles.

Later, he'll pay the tab (or what is more likely, I'll pay the tab). We'll walk over to the upscale martini bar so he can try to pick up the barmaid he met there last week. She'll giggle like she thinks he's funny, and he'll drink until he's sloppy. When we tip out, she'll go home with a waiter.

Later still, I'll walk Sasha through the back alleys of Westbrook. I'll shiver in the cold, and she'll sniff dumpsters. Then, we'll go home, turn out the lights, and climb onto our bed. We'll listen to the night. Winter is coming, and the dark hours last longer and longer.

Soon, I think, there will be no more daylight at all.

Acknowledgements

I am indebted to Christopher Pimental for his expertise. His explanation of the do's (and more importantly, the don'ts) of private investigation, along with his close reading, helped inform my novel. The idea of an amateur being more effective than a professional is amusing for a cozy mystery, but not for noir. Chris helped me map Slag's missteps.

Thanks also to my two critique groups, who suffered through two rounds of rewrites with these chapters.

My wife Judith, who has always been supportive of my writing, listened to me drone on about the philosophy behind noir over many, many beers (mine, not hers). Someday, people may light votive candles to the new patron saint of patience. Until then, thank you J.

Finally, thanks to Reagan and Black Rose Writing for their continued support. In a publishing field dominated by non-fiction, my little books sneak their noses under the big tent because of their mission

About the Author

Brian Kaufman is the author of ten novels, five textbooks, multiple study guides, and a collection of novellas. He lives with his wife and dog in the Colorado mountains. Kaufman divides his time between his various passions, including blues guitar, weightlifting, hiking, and book hoarding. Most of all, he writes.

Other Titles by Brian Kaufman

Note from Brian Kaufman

Word-of-mouth is crucial for any author to succeed. If you enjoyed *Rat Town Blues*, please leave a review online—anywhere you are able. Even if it's just a sentence or two. It would make all the difference and would be very much appreciated.

Thanks!
Brian Kaufman

We hope you enjoyed reading this title from:

www.blackrosewriting.com

Subscribe to our mailing list – *The Rosevine* – and receive **FREE** books, daily deals, and stay current with news about upcoming releases and our hottest authors.
Scan the QR code below to sign up.

Already a subscriber? Please accept a sincere thank you for being a fan of Black Rose Writing authors.

View other Black Rose Writing titles at www.blackrosewriting.com/books and use promo code **PRINT** to receive a **20% discount** when purchasing.